WAR AND PEACE
BOOK THREE : 1805

By Leo Tolstoy

War and Peace Book 3
by Leo Tolstoy

Copyright © 2025

All Rights reserved.
No part of this publication may be reproduced, stored in a retrieval system, or transmitted in any form or by any means, electronic, mechanical, photocopying or Otherwise, without the written permission of the publisher.

The author/editor asserts the moral right to be identified as the author/editor of this work.

ISBN: 978-93-94973-41-1

Published by
DOUBLE 9 BOOKS
2/13-B, Ansari Road
Daryaganj, New Delhi - 110002
info@double9books.com
www.double9books.com
Tel. 011-40042856

This book is under public domain

Printed in India.

About the Author

Leo Tolstoy was a Russian creator known for his books War and Peace which is viewed as the best book of pragmatist fiction. Tolstoy is additionally viewed as world's best author by quite a few people. Additionally an ethical scholar and a social reformer, Tolstoy had extreme moralistic points of view. In later life, he turned into an intense Christian rebel and anarcho-conservative.

Leo Tolstoy Born in Yasnaya Polyana on September 9, 1828, He had a place with a notable honorable Russian family. He was the fourth among five offspring of Count Nikolai Ilyich Tolstoy and Countess Mariya Tolstaya, both of whom kicked the bucket passing on their youngsters to be raised by family members.

In 1844, Tolstoy was acknowledged into Kazan University. Incapable to graduate past the subsequent year, Tolstoy got back to Yasnava Polyana and afterward invested energy going among Moscow and St. Petersburg. With some functioning information on a few dialects, he turned into a multilingual. Yet again the recently observed youth pulled in Tolstoy towards drinking, visiting massage parlors and most betting which left him in weighty obligation and anguish however Tolstoy before long acknowledged he was carrying on with a brutish life and endeavored college tests with the expectation that he would acquire a situation with the public authority, yet finished yet up in Caucuses serving in the military continuing in the strides of his senior sibling.

In Year 1862, Leo Tolstoy wedded Sophia Andreevna Behrs, generally called Sonya, who was 16 years more youthful than him. The couple had thirteen youngsters, of which, five passed on at an early age. Sonya went about as Tolstoy's secretary, editor and monetary chief while he made two out of his most prominent works. Their initial wedded life was loaded up with happiness.

He started composing his show-stopper, War and Peace in 1862. The six volumes of the work were distributed somewhere in the range of 1863 and 1869. With 580 characters got from history and others made by Tolstoy, this extraordinary novel takes on investigating the hypothesis of history and the irrelevance of noted figures like Alexander and Napoleon. Anna Karenina, Tolstoy's next epic was begun in 1873 and distributed totally in 1878.

Contents

BOOK THREE : 1805

CHAPTER I	9
CHAPTER II	17
CHAPTER III	25
CHAPTER IV	34
CHAPTER V	42
CHAPTER VI	48
CHAPTER VII	54
CHAPTER VIII	63
CHAPTER IX	68
CHAPTER X	74
CHAPTER XI	79
CHAPTER XII	83
CHAPTER XIII	89
CHAPTER XIV	95
CHAPTER XV	101
CHAPTER XVI	107
CHAPTER XVII	111
CHAPTER XVIII	117
CHAPTER XIX	124

BOOK THREE : 1805

CHAPTER I

Prince Vasíli was not a man who deliberately thought out his plans. Still less did he think of injuring anyone for his own advantage. He was merely a man of the world who had got on and to whom getting on had become a habit. Schemes and devices for which he never rightly accounted to himself, but which formed the whole interest of his life, were constantly shaping themselves in his mind, arising from the circumstances and persons he met. Of these plans he had not merely one or two in his head but dozens, some only beginning to form themselves, some approaching achievement, and some in course of disintegration. He did not, for instance, say to himself: "This man now has influence, I must gain his confidence and friendship and through him obtain a special grant." Nor did he say to himself: "Pierre is a rich man, I must entice him to marry my daughter and lend me the forty thousand rubles I need." But when he came across a man of position his instinct immediately told him that this man could be useful, and without any premeditation Prince Vasíli took the first opportunity to gain his confidence, flatter him, become intimate with him, and finally make his request.

He had Pierre at hand in Moscow and procured for him an appointment as Gentleman of the Bedchamber, which at that time conferred the status of Councilor of State, and insisted on the young man accompanying him to Petersburg and staying at his house. With apparent absent-mindedness, yet with unhesitating assurance that he was doing the right thing, Prince Vasíli did everything to get Pierre to marry his daughter. Had he thought out his plans beforehand he could not have been so natural and shown such unaffected familiarity in intercourse with everybody both above and below him in social standing. Something always drew him toward those richer and more powerful than himself and he had rare skill in seizing the most opportune moment for making use of people.

Pierre, on unexpectedly becoming Count Bezúkhov and a rich man, felt himself after his recent loneliness and freedom from cares so beset and preoccupied that only in bed was he able to be by himself. He had to sign papers, to present himself at government offices, the purpose of which was not clear to him, to question his chief steward, to visit his estate near Moscow, and to receive many people who formerly did not even wish to know of his existence but would now have been offended and grieved had he chosen not to see them. These different people—businessmen, relations, and acquaintances alike—were all disposed to treat the young heir in the most friendly and flattering manner: they were all evidently firmly convinced of Pierre's noble qualities. He was always hearing such words as: "With your remarkable kindness," or, "With your excellent heart," "You are yourself so honorable, Count," or, "Were he as clever as you," and so on, till he began sincerely to believe in his own exceptional kindness and extraordinary intelligence, the more so as in the depth of his heart it had always seemed to him that he really was very kind and intelligent. Even people who had formerly been spiteful toward him and evidently unfriendly now became gentle and affectionate. The angry eldest princess, with the long waist and hair plastered down like a doll's, had come into Pierre's room after the funeral. With drooping eyes and frequent blushes she told him she was very sorry about their past misunderstandings and did not now feel she had a right to ask him for anything, except only for permission, after the blow she had received, to remain for a few weeks longer in the house she so loved and where she had sacrificed so much. She could not refrain from weeping at these words. Touched that this statuesque princess could so change, Pierre took her hand and begged her forgiveness, without knowing what for. From that day the eldest princess quite changed toward Pierre and began knitting a striped scarf for him.

"Do this for my sake, *moncher*; after all, she had to put up with a great deal from the deceased," said Prince Vasíli to him, handing him a deed to sign for the princess' benefit.

Prince Vasíli had come to the conclusion that it was necessary to throw this bone—a bill for thirty thousand rubles—to the poor princess that it might not occur to her to speak of his share in the affair of the inlaid portfolio. Pierre signed the deed and after that the princess grew still kinder. The younger sisters also became affectionate to him, especially the youngest, the pretty one with the mole, who often made him feel confused by her smiles and her own confusion when meeting him.

It seemed so natural to Pierre that everyone should like him, and it would have seemed so unnatural had anyone disliked him, that he could not but believe in the sincerity of those around him. Besides, he had no time to ask himself whether these people were sincere or not. He was always busy and always felt in a state of mild and cheerful intoxication. He felt as though he were the center of some important and general movement; that something was constantly expected of him, that if he did not do it he would grieve and disappoint many people, but if he did this and that, all would be well; and he did what was demanded of him, but still that happy result always remained in the future.

More than anyone else, Prince Vasíli took possession of Pierre's affairs and of Pierre himself in those early days. From the death of Count Bezúkhov he did not let go his hold of the lad. He had the air of a man oppressed by business, weary and suffering, who yet would not, for pity's sake, leave this helpless youth who, after all, was the son of his old friend and the possessor of such enormous wealth, to the caprice of fate and the designs of rogues. During the few days he spent in Moscow after the death of Count Bezúkhov, he would call Pierre, or go to him himself, and tell him what ought to be done in a tone of weariness and assurance, as if he were adding every time: "You know I am overwhelmed with business and it is purely out of charity that I trouble myself about you, and you also know quite well that what I propose is the only thing possible."

"Well, my dear fellow, tomorrow we are off at last," said Prince Vasíli one day, closing his eyes and fingering Pierre's elbow, speaking as if he were saying something which had long since been agreed upon and could not now be altered. "We start tomorrow and I'm giving you a place in my carriage. I am very glad. All our important business here is now settled, and I ought to have been off long ago. Here is something I have received from the chancellor. I asked him for you, and you have been entered in the diplomatic corps and made a Gentleman of the Bedchamber. The diplomatic career now lies open before you."

Notwithstanding the tone of wearied assurance with which these words were pronounced, Pierre, who had so long been considering his career, wished to make some suggestion. But Prince Vasíli interrupted him in the special deep cooing tone, precluding the possibility of interrupting his speech, which he used in extreme cases when special persuasion was needed.

"*Mais, moncher*, I did this for my own sake, to satisfy my conscience, and there is nothing to thank me for. No one has ever complained yet of being too much loved; and besides, you are free, you could throw it up tomorrow. But you will see everything for yourself when you get to Petersburg. It is high time for you to get away from these terrible recollections." Prince Vasíli sighed. "Yes, yes, my boy. And my valet can go in your carriage. Ah! I was nearly forgetting," he added. "You know, *moncher*, your father and I had some accounts to settle, so I have received what was due from the Ryazán estate and will keep it; you won't require it. We'll go into the accounts later."

By "what was due from the Ryazán estate" Prince Vasíli meant several thousand rubles quitrent received from Pierre's peasants, which the prince had retained for himself.

In Petersburg, as in Moscow, Pierre found the same atmosphere of gentleness and affection. He could not refuse the post, or rather the rank (for he did nothing), that Prince Vasíli had procured for him, and acquaintances, invitations, and social occupations were so numerous that, even more than in Moscow, he felt a sense of bewilderment, bustle, and continual expectation of some good, always in front of him but never attained.

Of his former bachelor acquaintances many were no longer in Petersburg. The Guards had gone to the front; Dólokhov had been reduced to the ranks; Anatole was in the army somewhere in the provinces; Prince Andrew was abroad; so Pierre had not the opportunity to spend his nights as he used to like to spend them, or to open his mind by intimate talks with a friend older than himself and whom he respected. His whole time was taken up with dinners and balls and was spent chiefly at Prince Vasíli's house in the company of the stout princess, his wife, and his beautiful daughter Hélène.

Like the others, Anna PávlovnaSchérer showed Pierre the change of attitude toward him that had taken place in society.

Formerly in Anna Pávlovna's presence, Pierre had always felt that what he was saying was out of place, tactless and unsuitable, that remarks which seemed to him clever while they formed in his mind became foolish as soon as he uttered them, while on the contrary Hippolyte's stupidest remarks came out clever and apt. Now everything Pierre said was *charmant*. Even if Anna Pávlovna did not say so, he could see that she wished to and only refrained out of regard for his modesty.

In the beginning of the winter of 1805-6 Pierre received one of Anna Pávlovna's usual pink notes with an invitation to which was added: "You will find the beautiful Hélène here, whom it is always delightful to see."

When he read that sentence, Pierre felt for the first time that some link which other people recognized had grown up between himself and Hélène, and that thought both alarmed him, as if some obligation were being imposed on him which he could not fulfill, and pleased him as an entertaining supposition.

Anna Pávlovna's "At Home" was like the former one, only the novelty she offered her guests this time was not Mortemart, but a diplomatist fresh from Berlin with the very latest details of the Emperor Alexander's visit to Potsdam, and of how the two august friends had pledged themselves in an indissoluble alliance to uphold the cause of justice against the enemy of the human race. Anna Pávlovna received Pierre with a shade of melancholy, evidently relating to the young man's recent loss by the death of Count Bezúkhov (everyone constantly considered it a duty to assure Pierre that he was greatly afflicted by the death of the father he had hardly known), and her melancholy was just like the august melancholy she showed at the mention of her most august Majesty the Empress MáryaFëdorovna. Pierre felt flattered by this. Anna Pávlovna arranged the different groups in her drawing room with her habitual skill. The large group, in which were Prince Vasíli and the generals, had the benefit of the diplomat. Another group was at the tea table. Pierre wished to join the former, but Anna Pávlovna—who was in the excited condition of a commander on a battlefield to whom thousands of new and brilliant ideas occur which there is hardly time to put in action—seeing Pierre, touched his sleeve with her finger, saying:

"Wait a bit, I have something in view for you this evening." (She glanced at Hélène and smiled at her.) "My dear Hélène, be charitable to my poor aunt who adores you. Go and keep her company for ten minutes. And that it will not be too dull, here is the dear count who will not refuse to accompany you."

The beauty went to the aunt, but Anna Pávlovna detained Pierre, looking as if she had to give some final necessary instructions.

"Isn't she exquisite?" she said to Pierre, pointing to the stately beauty as she glided away. "And how she carries herself! For so young a girl, such tact, such masterly perfection of manner! It comes from her heart. Happy the man who wins her! With her the least worldly of men would occupy a most brilliant position in society. Don't you think so? I only wanted to know your opinion," and Anna Pávlovna let Pierre go.

Pierre, in reply, sincerely agreed with her as to Hélène's perfection of manner. If he ever thought of Hélène, it was just of her beauty and her remarkable skill in appearing silently dignified in society.

The old aunt received the two young people in her corner, but seemed desirous of hiding her adoration for Hélène and inclined rather to show her fear of Anna Pávlovna. She looked at her niece, as if inquiring what she was to do with these people. On leaving them, Anna Pávlovna again touched Pierre's sleeve, saying: "I hope you won't say that it is dull in my house again," and she glanced at Hélène.

Hélène smiled, with a look implying that she did not admit the possibility of anyone seeing her without being enchanted. The aunt coughed, swallowed, and said in French that she was very pleased to see Hélène, then she turned to Pierre with the same words of welcome and the same look. In the middle of a dull and halting conversation, Hélène turned to Pierre with the beautiful bright smile that she gave to everyone. Pierre was so used to that smile, and it had so little meaning for him, that he paid no attention to it. The aunt was just speaking of a collection of snuffboxes that had belonged to Pierre's father, Count Bezúkhov, and showed them her own box. Princess Hélène asked to see the portrait of the aunt's husband on the box lid.

"That is probably the work of Vinesse," said Pierre, mentioning a celebrated miniaturist, and he leaned over the table to take the snuffbox while trying to hear what was being said at the other table.

He half rose, meaning to go round, but the aunt handed him the snuffbox, passing it across Hélène's back. Hélène stooped forward to make room, and looked round with a smile. She was, as always at evening parties, wearing a dress such as was then fashionable, cut very low at front and back. Her bust, which had always seemed like marble to Pierre, was so close to him that his shortsighted eyes could not but perceive the living charm of her neck and shoulders, so near to his lips that he need only have bent his head a little to have touched them. He was conscious of the warmth of her body, the scent of perfume, and the creaking of her corset as she moved. He did not see her marble beauty forming a complete whole with her dress, but all the charm of her body only covered by her garments. And having once seen this he could not help being aware of it, just as we cannot renew an illusion we have once seen through.

"So you have never noticed before how beautiful I am?" Hélène seemed to say. "You had not noticed that I am a woman? Yes, I am a woman who may belong to anyone—to you too," said her glance. And at that moment Pierre felt that Hélène not only could, but must, be his wife, and that it could not be otherwise.

He knew this at that moment as surely as if he had been standing at the altar with her. How and when this would be he did not know, he did not even know if it would be a good thing (he even felt, he knew not why, that it would be a bad thing), but he knew it would happen.

Pierre dropped his eyes, lifted them again, and wished once more to see her as a distant beauty far removed from him, as he had seen her every day until then, but he could no longer do it. He could not, any more than a man who has been looking at a tuft of steppe grass through the mist and taking it for a tree can again take it for a tree after he has once recognized it to be a tuft of grass. She was terribly close to him. She already had power over him, and between them there was no longer any barrier except the barrier of his own will.

"Well, I will leave you in your little corner," came Anna Pávlovna's voice, "I see you are all right there."

And Pierre, anxiously trying to remember whether he had done anything reprehensible, looked round with a blush. It seemed to him that everyone knew what had happened to him as he knew it himself.

A little later when he went up to the large circle, Anna Pávlovna said to him: "I hear you are refitting your Petersburg house?"

This was true. The architect had told him that it was necessary, and Pierre, without knowing why, was having his enormous Petersburg house done up.

"That's a good thing, but don't move from Prince Vasíli's. It is good to have a friend like the prince," she said, smiling at Prince Vasíli. "I know something about that. Don't I? And you are still so young. You need advice. Don't be angry with me for exercising an old woman's privilege."

She paused, as women always do, expecting something after they have mentioned their age. "If you marry it will be a different thing," she continued, uniting them both in one glance. Pierre did not look at Hélène nor she at him. But she was just as terribly close to him. He muttered something and colored.

When he got home he could not sleep for a long time for thinking of what had happened. What had happened? Nothing. He had merely understood that the woman he had known as a child, of whom when her beauty was mentioned he had said absent-mindedly: "Yes, she's good looking," he had understood that this woman might belong to him.

"But she's stupid. I have myself said she is stupid," he thought. "There is something nasty, something wrong, in the feeling she excites in me. I have been told that her brother Anatole was in love with her and she with him, that there was quite a scandal and that that's why he was sent away. Hippolyte is her brother... Prince Vasíli is her father... It's bad...." he reflected, but while he was thinking this (the reflection was still incomplete), he caught himself smiling and was conscious that another line of thought had sprung up, and while thinking of her worthlessness he was also dreaming of how she would be his wife, how she would love him become quite different, and how all he had thought and heard of her might be false. And he again saw her not as the daughter of Prince Vasíli, but visualized her whole body only veiled by its gray dress. "But no! Why did this thought never occur to me before?" and again he told himself that it was impossible, that there would be something unnatural, and as it seemed to him dishonorable, in this marriage. He recalled her former words and looks and the words and looks of those who had seen them together. He recalled Anna Pávlovna's words and looks when she spoke to him about his house, recalled thousands of such hints from Prince Vasíli and others, and was seized by terror lest he had already, in some way, bound himself to do something that was evidently wrong and that he ought not to do. But at the very time he was expressing this conviction to himself, in another part of his mind her image rose in all its womanly beauty.

CHAPTER II

In November, 1805, Prince Vasíli had to go on a tour of inspection in four different provinces. He had arranged this for himself so as to visit his neglected estates at the same time and pick up his son Anatole where his regiment was stationed, and take him to visit Prince Nicholas Bolkónski in order to arrange a match for him with the daughter of that rich old man. But before leaving home and undertaking these new affairs, Prince Vasíli had to settle matters with Pierre, who, it is true, had latterly spent whole days at home, that is, in Prince Vasíli's house where he was staying, and had been absurd, excited, and foolish in Hélène's presence (as a lover should be), but had not yet proposed to her.

"This is all very fine, but things must be settled," said Prince Vasíli to himself, with a sorrowful sigh, one morning, feeling that Pierre who was under such obligations to him ("But never mind that") was not behaving very well in this matter. "Youth, frivolity... well, God be with him," thought he, relishing his own goodness of heart, "but it must be brought to a head. The day after tomorrow will be Lëlya's name day. I will invite two or three people, and if he does not understand what he ought to do then it will be my affair—yes, my affair. I am her father."

Six weeks after Anna Pávlovna's "At Home" and after the sleepless night when he had decided that to marry Hélène would be a calamity and that he ought to avoid her and go away, Pierre, despite that decision, had not left Prince Vasíli's and felt with terror that in people's eyes he was every day more and more connected with her, that it was impossible for him to return to his former conception of her, that he could not break away from her, and that though it would be a terrible thing he would have to unite his fate with hers. He might perhaps have been able to free himself but that Prince Vasíli (who had rarely before given receptions) now hardly let a day go by without having an evening party at which Pierre had to be present unless he wished to spoil the general pleasure and disappoint everyone's expectation. Prince Vasíli, in the rare moments when he was at home, would take Pierre's hand in passing and draw it downwards, or absent-mindedly hold out his wrinkled, clean-shaven cheek for Pierre to kiss and would say: "Till tomorrow," or, "Be in to dinner or I shall not see you," or, "I am staying in for your sake," and so on. And though Prince Vasíli, when he stayed in (as he said) for Pierre's sake, hardly exchanged a couple of words with him, Pierre felt unable to disappoint him. Every day he said to himself one and the same thing: "It is time I understood her and made up my mind what she really is. Was I mistaken before, or am I mistaken now? No, she is not stupid, she is an excellent girl," he sometimes said to himself "she never makes a mistake, never says anything stupid. She says little, but what she does say is always clear and simple, so she is not stupid. She never was abashed and is not abashed now, so she cannot be a bad woman!" He had often begun to make reflections or think aloud in her company, and she had always answered him either by a brief but appropriate remark—showing that it did not interest her—or by a silent look and smile which more palpably than anything else showed Pierre her superiority. She was right in regarding all arguments as nonsense in comparison with that smile.

She always addressed him with a radiantly confiding smile meant for him alone, in which there was something more significant than in the general smile that usually brightened her face. Pierre knew that everyone was waiting for him to say a word and cross a certain line, and he knew that sooner or later he would step across it, but an incomprehensible terror seized him at the thought of that dreadful step. A thousand times during that month and a half while he felt himself drawn nearer and nearer to that dreadful abyss, Pierre said to himself: "What am I doing? I need resolution. Can it be that I have none?"

He wished to take a decision, but felt with dismay that in this matter he lacked that strength of will which he had known in himself and really possessed. Pierre was one of those who are only strong when they feel themselves quite innocent, and since that day when he was overpowered by a feeling of desire while stooping over the snuffbox at Anna Pávlovna's, an unacknowledged sense of the guilt of that desire paralyzed his will.

On Hélène's name day, a small party of just their own people—as his wife said—met for supper at Prince Vasíli's. All these friends and relations had been given to understand that the fate of the young girl would be decided that evening. The visitors were seated at supper. Princess Kurágina, a portly imposing woman who had once been handsome, was sitting at the head of the table. On either side of her sat the more important guests—an old general and his wife, and Anna PávlovnaSchérer. At the other end sat the younger and less important guests, and there too sat the members of the family, and Pierre and Hélène, side by side. Prince Vasíli was not having any supper: he went round the table in a merry mood, sitting down now by one, now by another, of the guests. To each of them he made some careless and agreeable remark except to Pierre and Hélène, whose presence he seemed not to notice. He enlivened the whole party. The wax candles burned brightly, the silver and crystal gleamed, so did the ladies' toilets and the gold and silver of the men's epaulets; servants in scarlet liveries moved round the table, the clatter of plates, knives, and glasses mingled with the animated hum of several conversations. At one end of the table, the old chamberlain was heard assuring an old baroness that he loved her passionately, at which she laughed; at the other could be heard the story of the misfortunes of some Mary Víktorovna or other. At the center of the table, Prince Vasíli attracted everybody's attention. With a facetious smile on his face, he was telling the ladies about last Wednesday's meeting of the Imperial Council, at which SergéyKuzmíchVyazmítinov, the new military governor general of Petersburg, had received and read the then famous rescript of the Emperor Alexander from the army to SergéyKuzmích, in which the Emperor said that he was receiving from all sides declarations of the people's loyalty, that the declaration from Petersburg gave him particular pleasure, and that he was proud to be at the head of such a nation and would endeavor to be worthy of it. This rescript began with the words: "SergéyKuzmích, From all sides reports reach me," etc.

"Well, and so he never got farther than: 'SergéyKuzmích'?" asked one of the ladies.

"Exactly, not a hair's breadth farther," answered Prince Vasíli, laughing, "'SergéyKuzmích... From all sides... From all sides... SergéyKuzmích...' Poor Vyazmítinov could not get any farther! He began the rescript again and again, but as soon as he uttered *'Sergéy'* he sobbed, *'Kuz-mí-ch,'* tears, and *'From all sides'* was smothered in sobs and he could get no farther. And again his handkerchief, and again: 'SergéyKuzmích, From all sides,'... and tears, till at last somebody else was asked to read it."

"Kuzmích... From all sides... and then tears," someone repeated laughing.

"Don't be unkind," cried Anna Pávlovna from her end of the table holding up a threatening finger. "He is such a worthy and excellent man, our dear Vyazmítinov...."

Everybody laughed a great deal. At the head of the table, where the honored guests sat, everyone seemed to be in high spirits and under the influence of a variety of exciting sensations. Only Pierre and Hélène sat silently side by side almost at the bottom of the table, a suppressed smile brightening both their faces, a smile that had nothing to do with SergéyKuzmích—a smile of bashfulness at their own feelings. But much as all the rest laughed, talked, and joked, much as they enjoyed their Rhine wine, *sauté*, and ices, and however they avoided looking at the young couple, and heedless and unobservant as they seemed of them, one could feel by the occasional glances they gave that the story about SergéyKuzmích, the laughter, and the food were all a pretense, and that the whole attention of that company was directed to—Pierre and Hélène. Prince Vasíli mimicked the sobbing of SergéyKuzmích and at the same time his eyes glanced toward his daughter, and while he laughed the expression on his face clearly said: "Yes... it's getting on, it will all be settled today." Anna Pávlovna threatened him on behalf of "our dear Vyazmítinov," and in her eyes, which, for an instant, glanced at Pierre, Prince Vasíli read a congratulation on his future son-in-law and on his daughter's happiness. The old princess sighed sadly as she offered some wine to the old lady next to her and glanced angrily at her daughter, and her sigh seemed to say: "Yes, there's nothing left for you and me but to sip sweet wine, my dear, now that the time has come for these young ones to be thus boldly, provocatively happy." "And what nonsense all this is that I am saying!" thought a diplomatist, glancing at the happy faces of the lovers. "That's happiness!"

Into the insignificant, trifling, and artificial interests uniting that society had entered the simple feeling of the attraction of a healthy and handsome young man and woman for one another. And this human feeling dominated everything else and soared above all their affected chatter. Jests fell flat, news was not interesting, and the animation was evidently forced. Not only the guests but even the footmen waiting at table seemed to feel this, and they forgot their duties as they looked at the beautiful Hélène with her radiant face and at the red, broad, and happy though uneasy face of Pierre. It seemed as if the very light of the candles was focused on those two happy faces alone.

Pierre felt that he was the center of it all, and this both pleased and embarrassed him. He was like a man entirely absorbed in some occupation. He did not see, hear, or understand anything clearly. Only now and then detached ideas and impressions from the world of reality shot unexpectedly through his mind.

"So it is all finished!" he thought. "And how has it all happened? How quickly! Now I know that not because of her alone, nor of myself alone, but because of everyone, *it* must inevitably come about. They are all expecting *it*, they are so sure that it will happen that I cannot, I cannot, disappoint them. But how will it be? I do not know, but it will certainly happen!" thought Pierre, glancing at those dazzling shoulders close to his eyes.

Or he would suddenly feel ashamed of he knew not what. He felt it awkward to attract everyone's attention and to be considered a lucky man and, with his plain face, to be looked on as a sort of Paris possessed of a Helen. "But no doubt it always is and must be so!" he consoled himself. "And besides, what have I done to bring it about? How did it begin? I traveled from Moscow with Prince Vasíli. Then there was nothing. So why should I not stay at his house? Then I played cards with her and picked up her reticule and drove out with her. How did it begin, when did it all come about?" And here he was sitting by her side as her betrothed, seeing, hearing, feeling her nearness, her breathing, her movements, her beauty. Then it would suddenly seem to him that it was not she but he was so unusually beautiful, and that that was why they all looked so at him, and flattered by this general admiration he would expand his chest, raise his head, and rejoice at his good fortune. Suddenly he heard a familiar voice repeating something to him a second time. But Pierre was so absorbed that he did not understand what was said.

"I am asking you when you last heard from Bolkónski," repeated Prince Vasíli a third time. "How absent-minded you are, my dear fellow."

Prince Vasíli smiled, and Pierre noticed that everyone was smiling at him and Hélène. "Well, what of it, if you all know it?" thought Pierre. "What of it? It's the truth!" and he himself smiled his gentle childlike smile, and Hélène smiled too.

"When did you get the letter? Was it from Olmütz?" repeated Prince Vasíli, who pretended to want to know this in order to settle a dispute.

"How can one talk or think of such trifles?" thought Pierre.

"Yes, from Olmütz," he answered, with a sigh.

After supper Pierre with his partner followed the others into the drawing room. The guests began to disperse, some without taking leave of Hélène. Some, as if unwilling to distract her from an important occupation, came up to her for a moment and made haste to go away, refusing to let her see them off. The diplomatist preserved a mournful silence as he left the drawing room. He pictured the vanity of his diplomatic career in comparison with Pierre's happiness. The old general grumbled at his wife when she asked how his leg was. "Oh, the old fool," he thought. "That Princess Hélène will be beautiful still when she's fifty."

"I think I may congratulate you," whispered Anna Pávlovna to the old princess, kissing her soundly. "If I hadn't this headache I'd have stayed longer."

The old princess did not reply, she was tormented by jealousy of her daughter's happiness.

While the guests were taking their leave Pierre remained for a long time alone with Hélène in the little drawing room where they were sitting. He had often before, during the last six weeks, remained alone with her, but had never spoken to her of love. Now he felt that it was inevitable, but he could not make up his mind to take the final step. He felt ashamed; he felt that he was occupying someone else's place here beside Hélène. "This happiness is not for you," some inner voice whispered to him. "This happiness is for those who have not in them what there is in you."

But, as he had to say something, he began by asking her whether she was satisfied with the party. She replied in her usual simple manner that this name day of hers had been one of the pleasantest she had ever had.

Some of the nearest relatives had not yet left. They were sitting in the large drawing room. Prince Vasíli came up to Pierre with languid footsteps. Pierre rose and said it was getting late. Prince Vasíli gave him a look of stern inquiry, as though what Pierre had just said was so strange that one could not take it in. But then the expression of severity changed, and he drew Pierre's hand downwards, made him sit down, and smiled affectionately.

"Well, Lëlya?" he asked, turning instantly to his daughter and addressing her with the careless tone of habitual tenderness natural to parents who have petted their children from babyhood, but which Prince Vasíli had only acquired by imitating other parents.

And he again turned to Pierre.

"SergéyKuzmích—From all sides—" he said, unbuttoning the top button of his waistcoat.

Pierre smiled, but his smile showed that he knew it was not the story about SergéyKuzmích that interested Prince Vasíli just then, and Prince Vasíli saw that Pierre knew this. He suddenly muttered something and went away. It seemed to Pierre that even the prince was disconcerted. The sight of the discomposure of that old man of the world touched Pierre: he looked at Hélène and she too seemed disconcerted, and her look seemed to say: "Well, it is your own fault."

"The step must be taken but I cannot, I cannot!" thought Pierre, and he again began speaking about indifferent matters, about SergéyKuzmích, asking what the point of the story was as he had not heard it properly. Hélène answered with a smile that she too had missed it.

When Prince Vasíli returned to the drawing room, the princess, his wife, was talking in low tones to the elderly lady about Pierre.

"Of course, it is a very brilliant match, but happiness, my dear..."

"Marriages are made in heaven," replied the elderly lady.

Prince Vasíli passed by, seeming not to hear the ladies, and sat down on a sofa in a far corner of the room. He closed his eyes and seemed to be dozing. His head sank forward and then he roused himself.

"Aline," he said to his wife, "go and see what they are about."

The princess went up to the door, passed by it with a dignified and indifferent air, and glanced into the little drawing room. Pierre and Hélène still sat talking just as before.

"Still the same," she said to her husband.

Prince Vasíli frowned, twisting his mouth, his cheeks quivered and his face assumed the coarse, unpleasant expression peculiar to him. Shaking himself, he rose, threw back his head, and with resolute steps went past the ladies into the little drawing room. With quick steps he went joyfully up to Pierre. His face was so unusually triumphant that Pierre rose in alarm on seeing it.

"Thank God!" said Prince Vasíli. "My wife has told me everything!" (He put one arm around Pierre and the other around his daughter.)— "My dear boy... Lëlya... I am very pleased." (His voice trembled.) "I loved your father... and she will make you a good wife... God bless you!..."

He embraced his daughter, and then again Pierre, and kissed him with his malodorous mouth. Tears actually moistened his cheeks.

"Princess, come here!" he shouted.

The old princess came in and also wept. The elderly lady was using her handkerchief too. Pierre was kissed, and he kissed the beautiful Hélène's hand several times. After a while they were left alone again.

"All this had to be and could not be otherwise," thought Pierre, "so it is useless to ask whether it is good or bad. It is good because it's definite and one is rid of the old tormenting doubt." Pierre held the hand of his betrothed in silence, looking at her beautiful bosom as it rose and fell.

"Hélène!" he said aloud and paused.

"Something special is always said in such cases," he thought, but could not remember what it was that people say. He looked at her face. She drew nearer to him. Her face flushed.

"Oh, take those off... those..." she said, pointing to his spectacles.

Pierre took them off, and his eyes, besides the strange look eyes have from which spectacles have just been removed, had also a frightened and inquiring look. He was about to stoop over her hand and kiss it, but with a rapid, almost brutal movement of her head, she intercepted his lips and met them with her own. Her face struck Pierre, by its altered, unpleasantly excited expression.

"It is too late now, it's done; besides I love her," thought Pierre.

"Je vous aime!" * he said, remembering what has to be said at such moments: but his words sounded so weak that he felt ashamed of himself.

* "I love you."

Six weeks later he was married, and settled in Count Bezúkhov's large, newly furnished Petersburg house, the happy possessor, as people said, of a wife who was a celebrated beauty and of millions of money.

CHAPTER III

Old Prince Nicholas Bolkónski received a letter from Prince Vasíli in November, 1805, announcing that he and his son would be paying him a visit. "I am starting on a journey of inspection, and of course I shall think nothing of an extra seventy miles to come and see you at the same time, my honored benefactor," wrote Prince Vasíli. "My son Anatole is accompanying me on his way to the army, so I hope you will allow him personally to express the deep respect that, emulating his father, he feels for you."

"It seems that there will be no need to bring Mary out, suitors are coming to us of their own accord," incautiously remarked the little princess on hearing the news.

Prince Nicholas frowned, but said nothing.

A fortnight after the letter Prince Vasíli's servants came one evening in advance of him, and he and his son arrived next day.

Old Bolkónski had always had a poor opinion of Prince Vasíli's character, but more so recently, since in the new reigns of Paul and Alexander Prince Vasíli had risen to high position and honors. And now, from the hints contained in his letter and given by the little princess, he saw which way the wind was blowing, and his low opinion changed into a feeling of contemptuous ill will. He snorted whenever he mentioned him. On the day of Prince Vasíli's arrival, Prince Bolkónski was particularly discontented and out of temper. Whether he was in a bad temper because Prince Vasíli was coming, or whether his being in a bad temper made him specially annoyed at Prince Vasíli's visit, he was in a bad temper, and in the morning Tíkhon had already advised the architect not to go to the prince with his report.

"Do you hear how he's walking?" said Tíkhon, drawing the architect's attention to the sound of the prince's footsteps. "Stepping flat on his heels—we know what that means...."

However, at nine o'clock the prince, in his velvet coat with a sable collar and cap, went out for his usual walk. It had snowed the day before and the path to the hothouse, along which the prince was in the habit of walking, had been swept: the marks of the broom were still visible in the snow and a shovel had been left sticking in one of the soft snowbanks that bordered both sides of the path. The prince went through the conservatories, the serfs' quarters, and the outbuildings, frowning and silent.

"Can a sleigh pass?" he asked his overseer, a venerable man, resembling his master in manners and looks, who was accompanying him back to the house.

"The snow is deep. I am having the avenue swept, your honor."

The prince bowed his head and went up to the porch. "God be thanked," thought the overseer, "the storm has blown over!"

"It would have been hard to drive up, your honor," he added. "I heard, your honor, that a minister is coming to visit your honor."

The prince turned round to the overseer and fixed his eyes on him, frowning.

"What? A minister? What minister? Who gave orders?" he said in his shrill, harsh voice. "The road is not swept for the princess my daughter, but for a minister! For me, there are no ministers!"

"Your honor, I thought..."

"You thought!" shouted the prince, his words coming more and more rapidly and indistinctly. "You thought!... Rascals! Blackguards!... I'll teach you to think!" and lifting his stick he swung it and would have hit Alpátych, the overseer, had not the latter instinctively avoided the blow. "Thought... Blackguards..." shouted the prince rapidly.

But although Alpátych, frightened at his own temerity in avoiding the stroke, came up to the prince, bowing his bald head resignedly before him, or perhaps for that very reason, the prince, though he continued to shout: "Blackguards!... Throw the snow back on the road!" did not lift his stick again but hurried into the house.

Before dinner, Princess Mary and Mademoiselle Bourienne, who knew that the prince was in a bad humor, stood awaiting him; Mademoiselle Bourienne with a radiant face that said: "I know nothing, I am the same as usual," and Princess Mary pale, frightened, and with downcast eyes. What she found hardest to bear was to know that on such occasions she ought to behave like Mademoiselle Bourienne, but could not. She thought: "If I seem not to notice he will think that I do not sympathize with him; if I seem sad and out of spirits myself, he will say (as he has done before) that I'm in the dumps."

The prince looked at his daughter's frightened face and snorted.

"Fool... or dummy!" he muttered.

"And the other one is not here. They've been telling tales," he thought—referring to the little princess who was not in the dining room.

"Where is the princess?" he asked. "Hiding?"

"She is not very well," answered Mademoiselle Bourienne with a bright smile, "so she won't come down. It is natural in her state."

"Hm! Hm!" muttered the prince, sitting down.

His plate seemed to him not quite clean, and pointing to a spot he flung it away. Tíkhon caught it and handed it to a footman. The little princess was not unwell, but had such an overpowering fear of the prince that, hearing he was in a bad humor, she had decided not to appear.

"I am afraid for the baby," she said to Mademoiselle Bourienne: "Heaven knows what a fright might do."

In general at Bald Hills the little princess lived in constant fear, and with a sense of antipathy to the old prince which she did not realize because the fear was so much the stronger feeling. The prince reciprocated this antipathy, but it was overpowered by his contempt for her. When the little princess had grown accustomed to life at Bald Hills, she took a special fancy to Mademoiselle Bourienne, spent whole days with her, asked her to sleep in her room, and often talked with her about the old prince and criticized him.

"So we are to have visitors, *mon prince?*" remarked Mademoiselle Bourienne, unfolding her white napkin with her rosy fingers. "His Excellency Prince VasíliKurágin and his son, I understand?" she said inquiringly.

"Hm!—his excellency is a puppy.... I got him his appointment in the service," said the prince disdainfully. "Why his son is coming I don't understand. Perhaps Princess Elizabeth and Princess Mary know. I don't want him." (He looked at his blushing daughter.) "Are you unwell today? Eh? Afraid of the 'minister' as that idiot Alpátych called him this morning?"

"No, *monpère.*"

Though Mademoiselle Bourienne had been so unsuccessful in her choice of a subject, she did not stop talking, but chattered about the conservatories and the beauty of a flower that had just opened, and after the soup the prince became more genial.

After dinner, he went to see his daughter-in-law. The little princess was sitting at a small table, chattering with Másha, her maid. She grew pale on seeing her father-in-law.

She was much altered. She was now plain rather than pretty. Her cheeks had sunk, her lip was drawn up, and her eyes drawn down.

"Yes, I feel a kind of oppression," she said in reply to the prince's question as to how she felt.

"Do you want anything?"

"No, *merci, monpère.*"

"Well, all right, all right."

He left the room and went to the waiting room where Alpátych stood with bowed head.

"Has the snow been shoveled back?"

"Yes, your excellency. Forgive me for heaven's sake... It was only my stupidity."

"All right, all right," interrupted the prince, and laughing his unnatural way, he stretched out his hand for Alpátych to kiss, and then proceeded to his study.

Prince Vasíli arrived that evening. He was met in the avenue by coachmen and footmen, who, with loud shouts, dragged his sleighs up to one of the lodges over the road purposely laden with snow.

Prince Vasíli and Anatole had separate rooms assigned to them.

Anatole, having taken off his overcoat, sat with arms akimbo before a table on a corner of which he smilingly and absent-mindedly fixed his large and handsome eyes. He regarded his whole life as a continual round of amusement which someone for some reason had to provide for him. And he looked on this visit to a churlish old man and a rich and ugly heiress in the same way. All this might, he thought, turn out very well and amusingly. "And why not marry her if she really has so much money? That never does any harm," thought Anatole.

He shaved and scented himself with the care and elegance which had become habitual to him and, his handsome head held high, entered his father's room with the good-humored and victorious air natural to him. Prince Vasíli's two valets were busy dressing him, and he looked round with much animation and cheerfully nodded to his son as the latter entered, as if to say: "Yes, that's how I want you to look."

"I say, Father, joking apart, is she very hideous?" Anatole asked, as if continuing a conversation the subject of which had often been mentioned during the journey.

"Enough! What nonsense! Above all, try to be respectful and cautious with the old prince."

"If he starts a row I'll go away," said Prince Anatole. "I can't bear those old men! Eh?"

"Remember, for you everything depends on this."

In the meantime, not only was it known in the maidservants' rooms that the minister and his son had arrived, but the appearance of both had been minutely described. Princess Mary was sitting alone in her room, vainly trying to master her agitation.

"Why did they write, why did Lise tell me about it? It can never happen!" she said, looking at herself in the glass. "How shall I enter the drawing room? Even if I like him I can't now be myself with him." The mere thought of her father's look filled her with terror. The little princess and Mademoiselle Bourienne had already received from Másha, the lady's maid, the necessary report of how handsome the minister's son was, with his rosy cheeks and dark eyebrows, and with what difficulty the father had dragged his legs upstairs while the son had followed him like an eagle, three steps at a time. Having received this information, the little princess and Mademoiselle Bourienne, whose chattering voices had reached her from the corridor, went into Princess Mary's room.

"You know they've come, Marie?" said the little princess, waddling in, and sinking heavily into an armchair.

She was no longer in the loose gown she generally wore in the morning, but had on one of her best dresses. Her hair was carefully done and her face was animated, which, however, did not conceal its sunken and faded outlines. Dressed as she used to be in Petersburg society, it was still more noticeable how much plainer she had become. Some unobtrusive touch had been added to Mademoiselle Bourienne's toilet which rendered her fresh and pretty face yet more attractive.

"What! Are you going to remain as you are, dear princess?" she began. "They'll be announcing that the gentlemen are in the drawing room and we shall have to go down, and you have not smartened yourself up at all!"

The little princess got up, rang for the maid, and hurriedly and merrily began to devise and carry out a plan of how Princess Mary should be dressed. Princess Mary's self-esteem was wounded by the fact that the arrival of a suitor agitated her, and still more so by both her companions' not having the least conception that it could be otherwise. To tell them that she felt ashamed for herself and for them would be to betray her agitation, while to decline their offers to dress her would prolong their banter and insistence. She flushed, her beautiful eyes grew dim, red blotches came on her face, and it took on the unattractive martyrlike expression it so often wore, as she submitted herself to Mademoiselle Bourienne and Lise. Both these women *quite sincerely* tried to make her look pretty. She was so plain that neither of them could think of her as a rival, so they began dressing her with perfect sincerity, and with the naïve and firm conviction women have that dress can make a face pretty.

"No really, my dear, this dress is not pretty," said Lise, looking sideways at Princess Mary from a little distance. "You have a maroon dress, have it fetched. Really! You know the fate of your whole life may be at stake. But this one is too light, it's not becoming!"

It was not the dress, but the face and whole figure of Princess Mary that was not pretty, but neither Mademoiselle Bourienne nor the little princess felt this; they still thought that if a blue ribbon were placed in the hair, the hair combed up, and the blue scarf arranged lower on the best maroon dress, and so on, all would be well. They forgot that the frightened face and the figure could not be altered, and that however they might change the setting and adornment of that face, it would still remain piteous and plain. After two or three changes to which Princess Mary meekly submitted, just as her hair had been arranged on the top of her head (a style that quite altered and spoiled her looks) and she had put on a maroon dress with a pale-blue scarf, the little princess walked twice round her, now adjusting a fold of the dress with her little hand, now arranging the scarf and looking at her with her head bent first on one side and then on the other.

"No, it will not do," she said decidedly, clasping her hands. "No, Mary, really this dress does not suit you. I prefer you in your little gray everyday dress. Now please, do it for my sake. Katie," she said to the maid, "bring the princess her gray dress, and you'll see, Mademoiselle Bourienne, how I shall arrange it," she added, smiling with a foretaste of artistic pleasure.

But when Katie brought the required dress, Princess Mary remained sitting motionless before the glass, looking at her face, and saw in the mirror her eyes full of tears and her mouth quivering, ready to burst into sobs.

"Come, dear princess," said Mademoiselle Bourienne, "just one more little effort."

The little princess, taking the dress from the maid, came up to Princess Mary.

"Well, now we'll arrange something quite simple and becoming," she said.

The three voices, hers, Mademoiselle Bourienne's, and Katie's, who was laughing at something, mingled in a merry sound, like the chirping of birds.

"No, leave me alone," said Princess Mary.

Her voice sounded so serious and so sad that the chirping of the birds was silenced at once. They looked at the beautiful, large, thoughtful eyes full of tears and of thoughts, gazing shiningly and imploringly at them, and understood that it was useless and even cruel to insist.

"At least, change your coiffure," said the little princess. "Didn't I tell you," she went on, turning reproachfully to Mademoiselle Bourienne, "Mary's is a face which such a coiffure does not suit in the least. Not in the least! Please change it."

"Leave me alone, please leave me alone! It is all quite the same to me," answered a voice struggling with tears.

Mademoiselle Bourienne and the little princess had to own to themselves that Princess Mary in this guise looked very plain, worse than usual, but it was too late. She was looking at them with an expression they both knew, an expression thoughtful and sad. This expression in Princess Mary did not frighten them (she never inspired fear in anyone), but they knew that when it appeared on her face, she became mute and was not to be shaken in her determination.

"You will change it, won't you?" said Lise. And as Princess Mary gave no answer, she left the room.

Princess Mary was left alone. She did not comply with Lise's request, she not only left her hair as it was, but did not even look in her glass. Letting her arms fall helplessly, she sat with downcast eyes and pondered. A husband, a man, a strong dominant and strangely attractive being rose in her imagination, and carried her into a totally different happy world of his own. She fancied a child, *her own*—such as she had seen the day before in the arms of her nurse's daughter— at her own breast, the husband standing by and gazing tenderly at her and the child. "But no, it is impossible, I am too ugly," she thought.

"Please come to tea. The prince will be out in a moment," came the maid's voice at the door.

She roused herself, and felt appalled at what she had been thinking, and before going down she went into the room where the icons hung and, her eyes fixed on the dark face of a large icon of the Saviour lit by a lamp, she stood before it with folded hands for a few moments. A painful doubt filled her soul. Could the joy of love, of earthly love for a man, be for her? In her thoughts of marriage Princess Mary dreamed of happiness and of children, but her strongest, most deeply hidden longing was for earthly love. The more she tried to hide this feeling from others and even from herself, the stronger it grew. "O God," she said, "how am I to stifle in my heart these temptations of the devil? How am I to renounce forever these vile fancies, so as peacefully to fulfill Thy will?" And scarcely had she put that question than God gave her the answer in her own heart. "Desire nothing for thyself, seek nothing, be not anxious or envious. Man's future and thy own fate must remain hidden from thee, but live so that thou mayest be ready for anything. If it be God's will to prove thee in the duties of marriage, be ready to fulfill His will." With this consoling thought (but yet with a hope for the fulfillment of her forbidden earthly longing) Princess Mary sighed, and having crossed herself went down, thinking neither of her gown and coiffure nor of how she would go in nor of what she would say. What could all that matter in comparison with the will of God, without Whose care not a hair of man's head can fall?

CHAPTER IV

When Princess Mary came down, Prince Vasíli and his son were already in the drawing room, talking to the little princess and Mademoiselle Bourienne. When she entered with her heavy step, treading on her heels, the gentlemen and Mademoiselle Bourienne rose and the little princess, indicating her to the gentlemen, said: *"Voilà Marie!"* Princess Mary saw them all and saw them in detail. She saw Prince Vasíli's face, serious for an instant at the sight of her, but immediately smiling again, and the little princess curiously noting the impression "Marie" produced on the visitors. And she saw Mademoiselle Bourienne, with her ribbon and pretty face, and her unusually animated look which was fixed on *him*, but *him* she could not see, she only saw something large, brilliant, and handsome moving toward her as she entered the room. Prince Vasíli approached first, and she kissed the bold forehead that bent over her hand and answered his question by saying that, on the contrary, she remembered him quite well. Then Anatole came up to her. She still could not see him. She only felt a soft hand taking hers firmly, and she touched with her lips a white forehead, over which was beautiful light-brown hair smelling of pomade. When she looked up at him she was struck by his beauty. Anatole stood with his right thumb under a button of his uniform, his chest expanded and his back drawn in, slightly swinging one foot, and, with his head a little bent, looked with beaming face at the princess without speaking and evidently not thinking about her at all. Anatole was not quick-witted, nor ready or eloquent in conversation, but he had the faculty, so invaluable in society, of composure and imperturbable self-possession. If a man lacking in self-confidence remains dumb on a first introduction and betrays a consciousness of the impropriety of such silence and an anxiety to find something to say, the effect is bad. But Anatole was dumb, swung his foot, and smilingly examined the princess' hair. It was evident that he could be silent in this way for a very long time. "If anyone finds this silence inconvenient, let him talk, but I don't want to," he seemed to say. Besides this, in his behavior to women Anatole had a manner which particularly inspires in them curiosity, awe, and even love—a supercilious consciousness of his own superiority. It was as if he said to them: "I know you, I know you, but why should I bother about you? You'd be only too glad, of course." Perhaps he did not really think this when he met women—even probably he did not, for in general he thought very little—but his looks and manner gave that impression. The princess felt this, and as if wishing to show him that she did not even dare expect to interest him, she turned to his father. The conversation was general and animated, thanks to Princess Lise's voice and little downy lip that lifted over her white teeth. She met Prince Vasíli with that playful manner often employed by lively chatty people, and consisting in the assumption that between the person they so address and themselves there are some semi-private, long-established jokes and amusing reminiscences, though no such reminiscences really exist—just as none existed in this case. Prince Vasíli readily adopted her tone and the little princess also drew Anatole, whom she hardly knew, into these amusing recollections of things that had never occurred. Mademoiselle Bourienne also shared them and even Princess Mary felt herself pleasantly made to share in these merry reminiscences.

"Here at least we shall have the benefit of your company all to ourselves, dear prince," said the little princess (of course, in French) to Prince Vasíli. "It's not as at Annette's * receptions where you always ran away; you remember *cettechère Annette!*"

* Anna Pávlovna.

"Ah, but you won't talk politics to me like Annette!"

"And our little tea table?"

"Oh, yes!"

"Why is it you were never at Annette's?" the little princess asked Anatole. "Ah, I know, I know," she said with a sly glance, "your brother Hippolyte told me about your goings on. Oh!" and she shook her finger at him, "I have even heard of your doings in Paris!"

"And didn't Hippolyte tell you?" asked Prince Vasíli, turning to his son and seizing the little princess' arm as if she would have run away and he had just managed to catch her, "didn't he tell you how he himself was pining for the dear princess, and how she showed him the door? Oh, she is a pearl among women, Princess," he added, turning to Princess Mary.

When Paris was mentioned, Mademoiselle Bourienne for her part seized the opportunity of joining in the general current of recollections.

She took the liberty of inquiring whether it was long since Anatole had left Paris and how he had liked that city. Anatole answered the Frenchwoman very readily and, looking at her with a smile, talked to her about her native land. When he saw the pretty little Bourienne, Anatole came to the conclusion that he would not find Bald Hills dull either. "Not at all bad!" he thought, examining her, "not at all bad, that little companion! I hope she will bring her along with her when we're married, *la petite estgentille.*" *

* The little one is charming.

The old prince dressed leisurely in his study, frowning and considering what he was to do. The coming of these visitors annoyed him. "What are Prince Vasíli and that son of his to me? Prince Vasíli is a shallow braggart and his son, no doubt, is a fine specimen," he grumbled to himself. What angered him was that the coming of these visitors revived in his mind an unsettled question he always tried to stifle, one about which he always deceived himself. The question was whether he could ever bring himself to part from his daughter and give her to a husband. The prince never directly asked himself that question, knowing beforehand that he would have to answer it justly, and justice clashed not only with his feelings but with the very possibility of life. Life without Princess Mary, little as he seemed to value her, was unthinkable to him. "And why should she marry?" he thought. "To be unhappy for certain. There's Lise, married to Andrew—a better husband one would think could hardly be found nowadays—but is she contented with her lot? And who would marry Marie for love? Plain and awkward! They'll take her for her connections and wealth. Are there no women living unmarried, and even the happier for it?" So thought Prince Bolkónski while dressing, and yet the question he was always putting off demanded an immediate answer. Prince Vasíli had brought his son with the evident intention of proposing, and today or tomorrow he would probably ask for an answer. His birth and position in society were not bad. "Well, I've nothing against it," the prince said to himself, "but he must be worthy of her. And that is what we shall see."

"That is what we shall see! That is what we shall see!" he added aloud.

He entered the drawing room with his usual alert step, glancing rapidly round the company. He noticed the change in the little princess' dress, Mademoiselle Bourienne's ribbon, Princess Mary's unbecoming coiffure, Mademoiselle Bourienne's and Anatole's smiles, and the loneliness of his daughter amid the general conversation. "Got herself up like a fool!" he thought, looking irritably at her. "She is shameless, and he ignores her!"

He went straight up to Prince Vasíli.

"Well! How d'ye do? How d'ye do? Glad to see you!"

"Friendship laughs at distance," began Prince Vasíli in his usual rapid, self-confident, familiar tone. "Here is my second son; please love and befriend him."

Prince Bolkónski surveyed Anatole.

"Fine young fellow! Fine young fellow!" he said. "Well, come and kiss me," and he offered his cheek.

Anatole kissed the old man, and looked at him with curiosity and perfect composure, waiting for a display of the eccentricities his father had told him to expect.

Prince Bolkónski sat down in his usual place in the corner of the sofa and, drawing up an armchair for Prince Vasíli, pointed to it and began questioning him about political affairs and news. He seemed to listen attentively to what Prince Vasíli said, but kept glancing at Princess Mary.

"And so they are writing from Potsdam already?" he said, repeating Prince Vasíli's last words. Then rising, he suddenly went up to his daughter.

"Is it for visitors you've got yourself up like that, eh?" said he. "Fine, very fine! You have done up your hair in this new way for the visitors, and before the visitors I tell you that in future you are never to dare to change your way of dress without my consent."

"It was my fault, *monpère*," interceded the little princess, with a blush.

"You must do as you please," said Prince Bolkónski, bowing to his daughter-in-law, "but she need not make a fool of herself, she's plain enough as it is."

And he sat down again, paying no more attention to his daughter, who was reduced to tears.

"On the contrary, that coiffure suits the princess very well," said Prince Vasíli.

"Now you, young prince, what's your name?" said Prince Bolkónski, turning to Anatole, "come here, let us talk and get acquainted."

"Now the fun begins," thought Anatole, sitting down with a smile beside the old prince.

"Well, my dear boy, I hear you've been educated abroad, not taught to read and write by the deacon, like your father and me. Now tell me, my dear boy, are you serving in the Horse Guards?" asked the old man, scrutinizing Anatole closely and intently.

"No, I have been transferred to the line," said Anatole, hardly able to restrain his laughter.

"Ah! That's a good thing. So, my dear boy, you wish to serve the Tsar and the country? It is wartime. Such a fine fellow must serve. Well, are you off to the front?"

"No, Prince, our regiment has gone to the front, but I am attached… what is it I am attached to, Papa?" said Anatole, turning to his father with a laugh.

"A splendid soldier, splendid! 'What am I attached to!' Ha, ha, ha!" laughed Prince Bolkónski, and Anatole laughed still louder. Suddenly Prince Bolkónski frowned.

"You may go," he said to Anatole.

Anatole returned smiling to the ladies.

"And so you've had him educated abroad, Prince Vasíli, haven't you?" said the old prince to Prince Vasíli.

"I have done my best for him, and I can assure you the education there is much better than ours."

"Yes, everything is different nowadays, everything is changed. The lad's a fine fellow, a fine fellow! Well, come with me now." He took Prince Vasíli's arm and led him to his study. As soon as they were alone together, Prince Vasíli announced his hopes and wishes to the old prince.

"Well, do you think I shall prevent her, that I can't part from her?" said the old prince angrily. "What an idea! I'm ready for it tomorrow! Only let me tell you, I want to know my son-in-law better. You know my principles—everything aboveboard! I will ask her tomorrow in your presence; if she is willing, then he can stay on. He can stay and I'll see." The old prince snorted. "Let her marry, it's all the same to me!" he screamed in the same piercing tone as when parting from his son.

"I will tell you frankly," said Prince Vasíli in the tone of a crafty man convinced of the futility of being cunning with so keen-sighted a companion. "You know, you see right through people. Anatole is no genius, but he is an honest, goodhearted lad; an excellent son or kinsman."

"All right, all right, we'll see!"

As always happens when women lead lonely lives for any length of time without male society, on Anatole's appearance all the three women of Prince Bolkónski's household felt that their life had not been real till then. Their powers of reasoning, feeling, and observing immediately increased tenfold, and their life, which seemed to have been passed in darkness, was suddenly lit up by a new brightness, full of significance.

Princess Mary grew quite unconscious of her face and coiffure. The handsome open face of the man who might perhaps be her husband absorbed all her attention. He seemed to her kind, brave, determined, manly, and magnanimous. She felt convinced of that. Thousands of dreams of a future family life continually rose in her imagination. She drove them away and tried to conceal them.

"But am I not too cold with him?" thought the princess. "I try to be reserved because in the depth of my soul I feel too near to him already, but then he cannot know what I think of him and may imagine that I do not like him."

And Princess Mary tried, but could not manage, to be cordial to her new guest. "Poor girl, she's devilish ugly!" thought Anatole.

Mademoiselle Bourienne, also roused to great excitement by Anatole's arrival, thought in another way. Of course, she, a handsome young woman without any definite position, without relations or even a country, did not intend to devote her life to serving Prince Bolkónski, to reading aloud to him and being friends with Princess Mary. Mademoiselle Bourienne had long been waiting for a Russian prince who, able to appreciate at a glance her superiority to the plain, badly dressed, ungainly Russian princesses, would fall in love with her and carry her off; and here at last was a Russian prince. Mademoiselle Bourienne knew a story, heard from her aunt but finished in her own way, which she liked to repeat to herself. It was the story of a girl who had been seduced, and to whom her poor mother (*sapauvremère*) appeared, and reproached her for yielding to a man without being married. Mademoiselle Bourienne was often touched to tears as in imagination she told this story to *him*, her seducer. And now *he*, a real Russian prince, had appeared. He would carry her away and then *sapauvremère* would appear and he would marry her. So her future shaped itself in Mademoiselle Bourienne's head at the very time she was talking to Anatole about Paris. It was not calculation that guided her (she did not even for a moment consider what she should do), but all this had long been familiar to her, and now that Anatole had appeared it just grouped itself around him and she wished and tried to please him as much as possible.

The little princess, like an old war horse that hears the trumpet, unconsciously and quite forgetting her condition, prepared for the familiar gallop of coquetry, without any ulterior motive or any struggle, but with naïve and lighthearted gaiety.

Although in female society Anatole usually assumed the role of a man tired of being run after by women, his vanity was flattered by the spectacle of his power over these three women. Besides that, he was beginning to feel for the pretty and provocative Mademoiselle Bourienne that passionate animal feeling which was apt to master him with great suddenness and prompt him to the coarsest and most reckless actions.

After tea, the company went into the sitting room and Princess Mary was asked to play on the clavichord. Anatole, laughing and in high spirits, came and leaned on his elbows, facing her and beside Mademoiselle Bourienne. Princess Mary felt his look with a painfully joyous emotion. Her favorite sonata bore her into a most intimately poetic world and the look she felt upon her made that world still more poetic. But Anatole's expression, though his eyes were fixed on her, referred not to her but to the movements of Mademoiselle Bourienne's little foot, which he was then touching with his own under the clavichord. Mademoiselle Bourienne was also looking at Princess Mary, and in her lovely eyes there was a look of fearful joy and hope that was also new to the princess.

"How she loves me!" thought Princess Mary. "How happy I am now, and how happy I may be with such a friend and such a husband! Husband? Can it be possible?" she thought, not daring to look at his face, but still feeling his eyes gazing at her.

In the evening, after supper, when all were about to retire, Anatole kissed Princess Mary's hand. She did not know how she found the courage, but she looked straight into his handsome face as it came near to her shortsighted eyes. Turning from Princess Mary he went up and kissed Mademoiselle Bourienne's hand. (This was not etiquette, but then he did everything so simply and with such assurance!) Mademoiselle Bourienne flushed, and gave the princess a frightened look.

"What delicacy!" thought the princess. "Is it possible that Amélie" (Mademoiselle Bourienne) "thinks I could be jealous of her, and not value her pure affection and devotion to me?" She went up to her and kissed her warmly. Anatole went up to kiss the little princess' hand.

"No! No! No! When your father writes to tell me that you are behaving well I will give you my hand to kiss. Not till then!" she said. And smilingly raising a finger at him, she left the room.

CHAPTER V

They all separated, but, except Anatole who fell asleep as soon as he got into bed, all kept awake a long time that night.

"Is he really to be my husband, this stranger who is so kind—yes, kind, that is the chief thing," thought Princess Mary; and fear, which she had seldom experienced, came upon her. She feared to look round, it seemed to her that someone was there standing behind the screen in the dark corner. And this someone was *he*—the devil—and *he* was also this man with the white forehead, black eyebrows, and red lips.

She rang for her maid and asked her to sleep in her room.

Mademoiselle Bourienne walked up and down the conservatory for a long time that evening, vainly expecting someone, now smiling at someone, now working herself up to tears with the imaginary words of her *pauvremère* rebuking her for her fall.

The little princess grumbled to her maid that her bed was badly made. She could not lie either on her face or on her side. Every position was awkward and uncomfortable, and her burden oppressed her now more than ever because Anatole's presence had vividly recalled to her the time when she was not like that and when everything was light and gay. She sat in an armchair in her dressing jacket and nightcap and Katie, sleepy and disheveled, beat and turned the heavy feather bed for the third time, muttering to herself.

"I told you it was all lumps and holes!" the little princess repeated. "I should be glad enough to fall asleep, so it's not my fault!" and her voice quivered like that of a child about to cry.

The old prince did not sleep either. Tíkhon, half asleep, heard him pacing angrily about and snorting. The old prince felt as though he had been insulted through his daughter. The insult was the more pointed because it concerned not himself but another, his daughter, whom he loved more than himself. He kept telling himself that he would consider the whole matter and decide what was right and how he should act, but instead of that he only excited himself more and more.

"The first man that turns up—she forgets her father and everything else, runs upstairs and does up her hair and wags her tail and is unlike herself! Glad to throw her father over! And she knew I should notice it. Fr... fr... fr! And don't I see that that idiot had eyes only for Bourienne—I shall have to get rid of her. And how is it she has not pride enough to see it? If she has no pride for herself she might at least have some for my sake! She must be shown that the blockhead thinks nothing of her and looks only at Bourienne. No, she has no pride... but I'll let her see...."

The old prince knew that if he told his daughter she was making a mistake and that Anatole meant to flirt with Mademoiselle Bourienne, Princess Mary's self-esteem would be wounded and his point (not to be parted from her) would be gained, so pacifying himself with this thought, he called Tíkhon and began to undress.

"What devil brought them here?" thought he, while Tíkhon was putting the nightshirt over his dried-up old body and gray-haired chest. "I never invited them. They came to disturb my life—and there is not much of it left."

"Devil take 'em!" he muttered, while his head was still covered by the shirt.

Tíkhon knew his master's habit of sometimes thinking aloud, and therefore met with unaltered looks the angrily inquisitive expression of the face that emerged from the shirt.

"Gone to bed?" asked the prince.

Tíkhon, like all good valets, instinctively knew the direction of his master's thoughts. He guessed that the question referred to Prince Vasíli and his son.

"They have gone to bed and put out their lights, your excellency."

"No good... no good..." said the prince rapidly, and thrusting his feet into his slippers and his arms into the sleeves of his dressing gown, he went to the couch on which he slept.

Though no words had passed between Anatole and Mademoiselle Bourienne, they quite understood one another as to the first part of their romance, up to the appearance of the *pauvremère*; they understood that they had much to say to one another in private and so they had been seeking an opportunity since morning to meet one another alone. When Princess Mary went to her father's room at the usual hour, Mademoiselle Bourienne and Anatole met in the conservatory.

Princess Mary went to the door of the study with special trepidation. It seemed to her that not only did everybody know that her fate would be decided that day, but that they also knew what she thought about it. She read this in Tíkhon's face and in that of Prince Vasíli's valet, who made her a low bow when she met him in the corridor carrying hot water.

The old prince was very affectionate and careful in his treatment of his daughter that morning. Princess Mary well knew this painstaking expression of her father's. His face wore that expression when his dry hands clenched with vexation at her not understanding a sum in arithmetic, when rising from his chair he would walk away from her, repeating in a low voice the same words several times over.

He came to the point at once, treating her ceremoniously.

"I have had a proposition made me concerning you," he said with an unnatural smile. "I expect you have guessed that Prince Vasíli has not come and brought his pupil with him" (for some reason Prince Bolkónski referred to Anatole as a "pupil") "for the sake of my beautiful eyes. Last night a proposition was made me on your account and, as you know my principles, I refer it to you."

"How am I to understand you, *monpère?*" said the princess, growing pale and then blushing.

"How understand me!" cried her father angrily. "Prince Vasíli finds you to his taste as a daughter-in-law and makes a proposal to you on his pupil's behalf. That's how it's to be understood! 'How understand it'!... And I ask you!"

"I do not know what you think, Father," whispered the princess.

"I? I? What of me? Leave me out of the question. I'm not going to get married. What about *you?* That's what I want to know."

The princess saw that her father regarded the matter with disapproval, but at that moment the thought occurred to her that her fate would be decided now or never. She lowered her eyes so as not to see the gaze under which she felt that she could not think, but would only be able to submit from habit, and she said: "I wish only to do your will, but if I had to express my own desire..." She had no time to finish. The old prince interrupted her.

"That's admirable!" he shouted. "He will take you with your dowry and take Mademoiselle Bourienne into the bargain. She'll be the wife, while you..."

The prince stopped. He saw the effect these words had produced on his daughter. She lowered her head and was ready to burst into tears.

"Now then, now then, I'm only joking!" he said. "Remember this, Princess, I hold to the principle that a maiden has a full right to choose. I give you freedom. Only remember that your life's happiness depends on your decision. Never mind me!"

"But I do not know, Father!"

"There's no need to talk! He receives his orders and will marry you or anybody; but you are free to choose.... Go to your room, think it over, and come back in an hour and tell me in his presence: yes or no. I know you will pray over it. Well, pray if you like, but you had better *think* it over. Go! Yes or no, yes or no, yes or no!" he still shouted when the princess, as if lost in a fog, had already staggered out of the study.

Her fate was decided and happily decided. But what her father had said about Mademoiselle Bourienne was dreadful. It was untrue to be sure, but still it was terrible, and she could not help thinking of it. She was going straight on through the conservatory, neither seeing nor hearing anything, when suddenly the well-known whispering of Mademoiselle Bourienne aroused her. She raised her eyes, and two steps away saw Anatole embracing the Frenchwoman and whispering something to her. With a horrified expression on his handsome face, Anatole looked at Princess Mary, but did not at once take his arm from the waist of Mademoiselle Bourienne who had not yet seen her.

"Who's that? Why? Wait a moment!" Anatole's face seemed to say. Princess Mary looked at them in silence. She could not understand it. At last Mademoiselle Bourienne gave a scream and ran away. Anatole bowed to Princess Mary with a gay smile, as if inviting her to join in a laugh at this strange incident, and then shrugging his shoulders went to the door that led to his own apartments.

An hour later, Tíkhon came to call Princess Mary to the old prince; he added that Prince Vasíli was also there. When Tíkhon came to her Princess Mary was sitting on the sofa in her room, holding the weeping Mademoiselle Bourienne in her arms and gently stroking her hair. The princess' beautiful eyes with all their former calm radiance were looking with tender affection and pity at Mademoiselle Bourienne's pretty face.

"No, Princess, I have lost your affection forever!" said Mademoiselle Bourienne.

"Why? I love you more than ever," said Princess Mary, "and I will try to do all I can for your happiness."

"But you despise me. You who are so pure can never understand being so carried away by passion. Oh, only my poor mother..."

"I quite understand," answered Princess Mary, with a sad smile. "Calm yourself, my dear. I will go to my father," she said, and went out.

Prince Vasíli, with one leg thrown high over the other and a snuffbox in his hand, was sitting there with a smile of deep emotion on his face, as if stirred to his heart's core and himself regretting and laughing at his own sensibility, when Princess Mary entered. He hurriedly took a pinch of snuff.

"Ah, my dear, my dear!" he began, rising and taking her by both hands. Then, sighing, he added: "My son's fate is in your hands. Decide, my dear, good, gentle Marie, whom I have always loved as a daughter!"

He drew back and a real tear appeared in his eye.

"Fr... fr..." snorted Prince Bolkónski. "The prince is making a proposition to you in his pupil's—I mean, his son's—name. Do you wish or not to be Prince Anatole Kurágin's wife? Reply: yes or no," he shouted, "and then I shall reserve the right to state my opinion also. Yes, my opinion, and only my opinion," added Prince Bolkónski, turning to Prince Vasíli and answering his imploring look. "Yes, or no?"

"My desire is never to leave you, Father, never to separate my life from yours. I don't wish to marry," she answered positively, glancing at Prince Vasíli and at her father with her beautiful eyes.

"Humbug! Nonsense! Humbug, humbug, humbug!" cried Prince Bolkónski, frowning and taking his daughter's hand; he did not kiss her, but only bending his forehead to hers just touched it, and pressed her hand so that she winced and uttered a cry.

Prince Vasíli rose.

"My dear, I must tell you that this is a moment I shall never, never forget. But, my dear, will you not give us a little hope of touching this heart, so kind and generous? Say 'perhaps'... The future is so long. Say 'perhaps.'"

"Prince, what I have said is all there is in my heart. I thank you for the honor, but I shall never be your son's wife."

"Well, so that's finished, my dear fellow! I am very glad to have seen you. Very glad! Go back to your rooms, Princess. Go!" said the old prince. "Very, very glad to have seen you," repeated he, embracing Prince Vasíli.

"My vocation is a different one," thought Princess Mary. "My vocation is to be happy with another kind of happiness, the happiness of love and self-sacrifice. And cost what it may, I will arrange poor Amélie's happiness, she loves him so passionately, and so passionately repents. I will do all I can to arrange the match between them. If he is not rich I will give her the means; I will ask my father and Andrew. I shall be so happy when she is his wife. She is so unfortunate, a stranger, alone, helpless! And, oh God, how passionately she must love him if she could so far forget herself! Perhaps I might have done the same!..." thought Princess Mary.

CHAPTER VI

It was long since the Rostóvs had news of Nicholas. Not till midwinter was the count at last handed a letter addressed in his son's handwriting. On receiving it, he ran on tiptoe to his study in alarm and haste, trying to escape notice, closed the door, and began to read the letter.

Anna Mikháylovna, who always knew everything that passed in the house, on hearing of the arrival of the letter went softly into the room and found the count with it in his hand, sobbing and laughing at the same time.

Anna Mikháylovna, though her circumstances had improved, was still living with the Rostóvs.

"My dear friend?" said she, in a tone of pathetic inquiry, prepared to sympathize in any way.

The count sobbed yet more.

"Nikólenka... a letter... wa... a... s... wounded... my darling boy... the countess... promoted to be an officer... thank God... How tell the little countess!"

Anna Mikháylovna sat down beside him, with her own handkerchief wiped the tears from his eyes and from the letter, then having dried her own eyes she comforted the count, and decided that at dinner and till teatime she would prepare the countess, and after tea, with God's help, would inform her.

At dinner Anna Mikháylovna talked the whole time about the war news and about Nikólenka, twice asked when the last letter had been received from him, though she knew that already, and remarked that they might very likely be getting a letter from him that day. Each time that these hints began to make the countess anxious and she glanced uneasily at the count and at Anna Mikháylovna, the latter very adroitly turned the conversation to insignificant matters. Natásha, who, of the whole family, was the most gifted with a capacity to feel any shades of intonation, look, and expression, pricked up her ears from the beginning of the meal and was certain that there was some secret between her father and Anna Mikháylovna, that it had something to do with her brother, and that Anna Mikháylovna was preparing them for it. Bold as she was, Natásha, who knew how sensitive her mother was to anything relating to Nikólenka, did not venture to ask any questions at dinner, but she was too excited to eat anything and kept wriggling about on her chair regardless of her governess' remarks. After dinner, she rushed headlong after Anna Mikháylovna and, dashing at her, flung herself on her neck as soon as she overtook her in the sitting room.

"Auntie, darling, do tell me what it is!"

"Nothing, my dear."

"No, dearest, sweet one, honey, I won't give up—I know you know something."

Anna Mikháylovna shook her head.

"You are a little slyboots," she said.

"A letter from Nikólenka! I'm sure of it!" exclaimed Natásha, reading confirmation in Anna Mikháylovna's face.

"But for God's sake, be careful, you know how it may affect your mamma."

"I will, I will, only tell me! You won't? Then I will go and tell at once."

Anna Mikháylovna, in a few words, told her the contents of the letter, on condition that she should tell no one.

"No, on my true word of honor," said Natásha, crossing herself, "I won't tell anyone!" and she ran off at once to Sónya.

"Nikólenka... wounded... a letter," she announced in gleeful triumph.

"*Nicholas!*" was all Sónya said, instantly turning white.

Natásha, seeing the impression the news of her brother's wound produced on Sónya, felt for the first time the sorrowful side of the news.

She rushed to Sónya, hugged her, and began to cry.

"A little wound, but he has been made an officer; he is well now, he wrote himself," said she through her tears.

"There now! It's true that all you women are crybabies," remarked Pétya, pacing the room with large, resolute strides. "Now I'm very glad, very glad indeed, that my brother has distinguished himself so. You are all blubberers and understand nothing."

Natásha smiled through her tears.

"You haven't read the letter?" asked Sónya.

"No, but she said that it was all over and that he's now an officer."

"Thank God!" said Sónya, crossing herself. "But perhaps she deceived you. Let us go to Mamma."

Pétya paced the room in silence for a time.

"If I'd been in Nikólenka's place I would have killed even more of those Frenchmen," he said. "What nasty brutes they are! I'd have killed so many that there'd have been a heap of them."

"Hold your tongue, Pétya, what a goose you are!"

"I'm not a goose, but they are who cry about trifles," said Pétya.

"Do you remember him?" Natásha suddenly asked, after a moment's silence.

Sónya smiled.

"Do I remember *Nicholas?*"

"No, Sónya, but do you remember so that you remember him perfectly, remember everything?" said Natásha, with an expressive gesture, evidently wishing to give her words a very definite meaning. "I remember Nikólenka too, I remember him well," she said. "But I don't remember Borís. I don't remember him a bit."

"What! You don't remember Borís?" asked Sónya in surprise.

"It's not that I don't remember—I know what he is like, but not as I remember Nikólenka. Him—I just shut my eyes and remember, but Borís... No!" (She shut her eyes.) "No! there's nothing at all."

"Oh, Natásha!" said Sónya, looking ecstatically and earnestly at her friend as if she did not consider her worthy to hear what she meant to say and as if she were saying it to someone else, with whom joking was out of the question, "I am in love with your brother once for all and, whatever may happen to him or to me, shall never cease to love him as long as I live."

Natásha looked at Sónya with wondering and inquisitive eyes, and said nothing. She felt that Sónya was speaking the truth, that there was such love as Sónya was speaking of. But Natásha had not yet felt anything like it. She believed it could be, but did not understand it.

"Shall you write to him?" she asked.

Sónya became thoughtful. The question of how to write to *Nicholas*, and whether she ought to write, tormented her. Now that he was already an officer and a wounded hero, would it be right to remind him of herself and, as it might seem, of the obligations to her he had taken on himself?

"I don't know. I think if he writes, I will write too," she said, blushing.

"And you won't feel ashamed to write to him?"

Sónya smiled.

"No."

"And I should be ashamed to write to Borís. I'm not going to."

"Why should you be ashamed?"

"Well, I don't know. It's awkward and would make me ashamed."

"And I know why she'd be ashamed," said Pétya, offended by Natásha's previous remark. "It's because she was in love with that fat one in spectacles" (that was how Pétya described his namesake, the new Count Bezúkhov) "and now she's in love with that singer" (he meant Natásha's Italian singing master), "that's why she's ashamed!"

"Pétya, you're stupid!" said Natásha.

"Not more stupid than you, madam," said the nine-year-old Pétya, with the air of an old brigadier.

The countess had been prepared by Anna Mikháylovna's hints at dinner. On retiring to her own room, she sat in an armchair, her eyes fixed on a miniature portrait of her son on the lid of a snuffbox, while the tears kept coming into her eyes. Anna Mikháylovna, with the letter, came on tiptoe to the countess' door and paused.

"Don't come in," she said to the old count who was following her. "Come later." And she went in, closing the door behind her.

The count put his ear to the keyhole and listened.

At first he heard the sound of indifferent voices, then Anna Mikháylovna's voice alone in a long speech, then a cry, then silence, then both voices together with glad intonations, and then footsteps.

Anna Mikháylovna opened the door. Her face wore the proud expression of a surgeon who has just performed a difficult operation and admits the public to appreciate his skill.

"It is done!" she said to the count, pointing triumphantly to the countess, who sat holding in one hand the snuffbox with its portrait and in the other the letter, and pressing them alternately to her lips.

When she saw the count, she stretched out her arms to him, embraced his bald head, over which she again looked at the letter and the portrait, and in order to press them again to her lips, she slightly pushed away the bald head. Véra, Natásha, Sónya, and Pétya now entered the room, and the reading of the letter began. After a brief description of the campaign and the two battles in which he had taken part, and his promotion, Nicholas said that he kissed his father's and mother's hands asking for their blessing, and that he kissed Véra, Natásha, and Pétya. Besides that, he sent greetings to Monsieur Schelling, Madame Schoss, and his old nurse, and asked them to kiss for him "dear Sónya, whom he loved and thought of just the same as ever." When she heard this Sónya blushed so that tears came into her eyes and, unable to bear the looks turned upon her, ran away into the dancing hall, whirled round it at full speed with her dress puffed out like a balloon, and, flushed and smiling, plumped down on the floor. The countess was crying.

"Why are you crying, Mamma?" asked Véra. "From all he says one should be glad and not cry."

This was quite true, but the count, the countess, and Natásha looked at her reproachfully. "And who is it she takes after?" thought the countess.

Nicholas' letter was read over hundreds of times, and those who were considered worthy to hear it had to come to the countess, for she did not let it out of her hands. The tutors came, and the nurses, and Dmítri, and several acquaintances, and the countess reread the letter each time with fresh pleasure and each time discovered in it fresh proofs of Nikólenka's virtues. How strange, how extraordinary, how joyful it seemed, that her son, the scarcely perceptible motion of whose tiny limbs she had felt twenty years ago within her, that son about whom she used to have quarrels with the too indulgent count, that son who had first learned to say "pear" and then "granny," that this son should now be away in a foreign land amid strange surroundings, a manly warrior doing some kind of man's work of his own, without help or guidance. The universal experience of ages, showing that children do grow imperceptibly from the cradle to manhood, did not exist for the countess. Her son's growth toward manhood, at each of its stages, had seemed as extraordinary to her as if there had never existed the millions of human beings who grew up in the same way. As twenty years before, it seemed impossible that the little creature who lived somewhere under her heart would ever cry, suck her breast, and begin to speak, so now she could not believe that that little creature could be this strong, brave man, this model son and officer that, judging by this letter, he now was.

"What a *style!* How charmingly he describes!" said she, reading the descriptive part of the letter. "And what a soul! Not a word about himself.... Not a word! About some Denísov or other, though he himself, I dare say, is braver than any of them. He says nothing about his sufferings. What a heart! How like him it is! And how he has remembered everybody! Not forgetting anyone. I always said when he was only so high—I always said...."

For more than a week preparations were being made, rough drafts of letters to Nicholas from all the household were written and copied out, while under the supervision of the countess and the solicitude of the count, money and all things necessary for the uniform and equipment of the newly commissioned officer were collected. Anna Mikháylovna, practical woman that she was, had even managed by favor with army authorities to secure advantageous means of communication for herself and her son. She had opportunities of sending her letters to the Grand Duke Constantine Pávlovich, who commanded the Guards. The Rostóvs supposed that *The Russian Guards, Abroad*, was quite a definite address, and that if a letter reached the Grand Duke in command of the Guards there was no reason why it should not reach the Pávlograd regiment, which was presumably somewhere in the same neighborhood. And so it was decided to send the letters and money by the Grand Duke's courier to Borís and Borís was to forward them to Nicholas. The letters were from the old count, the countess, Pétya, Véra, Natásha, and Sónya, and finally there were six thousand rubles for his outfit and various other things the old count sent to his son.

CHAPTER VII

On the twelfth of November, Kutúzov's active army, in camp before Olmütz, was preparing to be reviewed next day by the two Emperors—the Russian and the Austrian. The Guards, just arrived from Russia, spent the night ten miles from Olmütz and next morning were to come straight to the review, reaching the field at Olmütz by ten o'clock.

That day Nicholas Rostóv received a letter from Borís, telling him that the Ismáylov regiment was quartered for the night ten miles from Olmütz and that he wanted to see him as he had a letter and money for him. Rostóv was particularly in need of money now that the troops, after their active service, were stationed near Olmütz and the camp swarmed with well-provisioned sutlers and Austrian Jews offering all sorts of tempting wares. The Pávlograds held feast after feast, celebrating awards they had received for the campaign, and made expeditions to Olmütz to visit a certain Caroline the Hungarian, who had recently opened a restaurant there with girls as waitresses. Rostóv, who had just celebrated his promotion to a cornetcy and bought Denísov's horse, Bedouin, was in debt all round, to his comrades and the sutlers. On receiving Borís' letter he rode with a fellow officer to Olmütz, dined there, drank a bottle of wine, and then set off alone to the Guards' camp to find his old playmate. Rostóv had not yet had time to get his uniform. He had on a shabby cadet jacket, decorated with a soldier's cross, equally shabby cadet's riding breeches lined with worn leather, and an officer's saber with a sword knot. The Don horse he was riding was one he had bought from a Cossack during the campaign, and he wore a crumpled hussar cap stuck jauntily back on one side of his head. As he rode up to the camp he thought how he would impress Borís and all his comrades of the Guards by his appearance—that of a fighting hussar who had been under fire.

The Guards had made their whole march as if on a pleasure trip, parading their cleanliness and discipline. They had come by easy stages, their knapsacks conveyed on carts, and the Austrian authorities had provided excellent dinners for the officers at every halting place. The regiments had entered and left the town with their bands playing, and by the Grand Duke's orders the men had marched all the way in step (a practice on which the Guards prided themselves), the officers on foot and at their proper posts. Borís had been quartered, and had marched all the way, with Berg who was already in command of a company. Berg, who had obtained his captaincy during the campaign, had gained the confidence of his superiors by his promptitude and accuracy and had arranged his money matters very satisfactorily. Borís, during the campaign, had made the acquaintance of many persons who might prove useful to him, and by a letter of recommendation he had brought from Pierre had become acquainted with Prince Andrew Bolkónski, through whom he hoped to obtain a post on the commander in chief's staff. Berg and Borís, having rested after yesterday's march, were sitting, clean and neatly dressed, at a round table in the clean quarters allotted to them, playing chess. Berg held a smoking pipe between his knees. Borís, in the accurate way characteristic of him, was building a little pyramid of chessmen with his delicate white fingers while awaiting Berg's move, and watched his opponent's face, evidently thinking about the game as he always thought only of whatever he was engaged on.

"Well, how are you going to get out of that?" he remarked.

"We'll try to," replied Berg, touching a pawn and then removing his hand.

At that moment the door opened.

"Here he is at last!" shouted Rostóv. "And Berg too! Oh, you *petisenfans, allay cushaydormir!*" he exclaimed, imitating his Russian nurse's French, at which he and Borís used to laugh long ago.

"Dear me, how you have changed!"

Borís rose to meet Rostóv, but in doing so did not omit to steady and replace some chessmen that were falling. He was about to embrace his friend, but Nicholas avoided him. With that peculiar feeling of youth, that dread of beaten tracks, and wish to express itself in a manner different from that of its elders which is often insincere, Nicholas wished to do something special on meeting his friend. He wanted to pinch him, push him, do anything but kiss him—a thing everybody did. But notwithstanding this, Borís embraced him in a quiet, friendly way and kissed him three times.

They had not met for nearly half a year and, being at the age when young men take their first steps on life's road, each saw immense changes in the other, quite a new reflection of the society in which they had taken those first steps. Both had changed greatly since they last met and both were in a hurry to show the changes that had taken place in them.

"Oh, you damned dandies! Clean and fresh as if you'd been to a fete, not like us sinners of the line," cried Rostóv, with martial swagger and with baritone notes in his voice, new to Borís, pointing to his own mud-bespattered breeches. The German landlady, hearing Rostóv's loud voice, popped her head in at the door.

"Eh, is she pretty?" he asked with a wink.

"Why do you shout so? You'll frighten them!" said Borís. "I did not expect you today," he added. "I only sent you the note yesterday by Bolkónski—an adjutant of Kutúzov's, who's a friend of mine. I did not think he would get it to you so quickly.... Well, how are you? Been under fire already?" asked Borís.

Without answering, Rostóv shook the soldier's Cross of St. George fastened to the cording of his uniform and, indicating a bandaged arm, glanced at Berg with a smile.

"As you see," he said.

"Indeed? Yes, yes!" said Borís, with a smile. "And we too have had a splendid march. You know, of course, that His Imperial Highness rode with our regiment all the time, so that we had every comfort and every advantage. What receptions we had in Poland! What dinners and balls! I can't tell you. And the Tsarévich was very gracious to all our officers."

And the two friends told each other of their doings, the one of his hussar revels and life in the fighting line, the other of the pleasures and advantages of service under members of the Imperial family.

"Oh, you Guards!" said Rostóv. "I say, send for some wine."

Borís made a grimace.

"If you really want it," said he.

He went to his bed, drew a purse from under the clean pillow, and sent for wine.

"Yes, and I have some money and a letter to give you," he added.

Rostóv took the letter and, throwing the money on the sofa, put both arms on the table and began to read. After reading a few lines, he glanced angrily at Berg, then, meeting his eyes, hid his face behind the letter.

"Well, they've sent you a tidy sum," said Berg, eying the heavy purse that sank into the sofa. "As for us, Count, we get along on our pay. I can tell you for myself..."

"I say, Berg, my dear fellow," said Rostóv, "when you get a letter from home and meet one of your own people whom you want to talk everything over with, and I happen to be there, I'll go at once, to be out of your way! Do go somewhere, anywhere... to the devil!" he exclaimed, and immediately seizing him by the shoulder and looking amiably into his face, evidently wishing to soften the rudeness of his words, he added, "Don't be hurt, my dear fellow; you know I speak from my heart as to an old acquaintance."

"Oh, don't mention it, Count! I quite understand," said Berg, getting up and speaking in a muffled and guttural voice.

"Go across to our hosts: they invited you," added Borís.

Berg put on the cleanest of coats, without a spot or speck of dust, stood before a looking glass and brushed the hair on his temples upwards, in the way affected by the Emperor Alexander, and, having assured himself from the way Rostóv looked at it that his coat had been noticed, left the room with a pleasant smile.

"Oh dear, what a beast I am!" muttered Rostóv, as he read the letter.

"Why?"

"Oh, what a pig I am, not to have written and to have given them such a fright! Oh, what a pig I am!" he repeated, flushing suddenly. "Well, have you sent Gabriel for some wine? All right let's have some!"

In the letter from his parents was enclosed a letter of recommendation to Bagratión which the old countess at Anna

Mikháylovna's advice had obtained through an acquaintance and sent to her son, asking him to take it to its destination and make use of it.

"What nonsense! Much I need it!" said Rostóv, throwing the letter under the table.

"Why have you thrown that away?" asked Borís.

"It is some letter of recommendation... what the devil do I want it for!"

"Why 'What the devil'?" said Borís, picking it up and reading the address. "This letter would be of great use to you."

"I want nothing, and I won't be anyone's adjutant."

"Why not?" inquired Borís.

"It's a lackey's job!"

"You are still the same dreamer, I see," remarked Borís, shaking his head.

"And you're still the same diplomatist! But that's not the point... Come, how are you?" asked Rostóv.

"Well, as you see. So far everything's all right, but I confess I should much like to be an adjutant and not remain at the front."

"Why?"

"Because when once a man starts on military service, he should try to make as successful a career of it as possible."

"Oh, that's it!" said Rostóv, evidently thinking of something else.

He looked intently and inquiringly into his friend's eyes, evidently trying in vain to find the answer to some question.

Old Gabriel brought in the wine.

"Shouldn't we now send for Berg?" asked Borís. "He would drink with you. I can't."

"Well, send for him... and how do you get on with that German?" asked Rostóv, with a contemptuous smile.

"He is a very, very nice, honest, and pleasant fellow," answered Borís.

AgainRostóv looked intently into Borís' eyes and sighed. Berg returned, and over the bottle of wine conversation between the three officers became animated. The Guardsmen told Rostóv of their march and how they had been made much of in Russia, Poland, and abroad. They spoke of the sayings and doings of their commander, the Grand Duke, and told stories of his kindness and irascibility. Berg, as usual, kept silent when the subject did not relate to himself, but in connection with the stories of the Grand Duke's quick temper he related with gusto how in Galicia he had managed to deal with the Grand Duke when the latter made a tour of the regiments and was annoyed at the irregularity of a movement. With a pleasant smile Berg related how the Grand Duke had ridden up to him in a violent passion, shouting: "Arnauts!" ("Arnauts" was the Tsarévich's favorite expression when he was in a rage) and called for the company commander.

"Would you believe it, Count, I was not at all alarmed, because I knew I was right. Without boasting, you know, I may say that I know the Army Orders by heart and know the Regulations as well as I do the Lord's Prayer. So, Count, there never is any negligence in my company, and so my conscience was at ease. I came forward...." (Berg stood up and showed how he presented himself, with his hand to his cap, and really it would have been difficult for a face to express greater respect and self-complacency than his did.) "Well, he stormed at me, as the saying is, stormed and stormed and stormed! It was not a matter of life but rather of death, as the saying is. 'Albanians!' and 'devils!' and 'To Siberia!'" said Berg with a sagacious smile. "I knew I was in the right so I kept silent; was not that best, Count?... 'Hey, are you dumb?' he shouted. Still I remained silent. And what do you think, Count? The next day it was not even mentioned in the Orders of the Day. That's what keeping one's head means. That's the way, Count," said Berg, lighting his pipe and emitting rings of smoke.

"Yes, that was fine," said Rostóv, smiling.

But Borís noticed that he was preparing to make fun of Berg, and skillfully changed the subject. He asked him to tell them how and where he got his wound. This pleased Rostóv and he began talking about it, and as he went on became more and more animated. He told them of his Schön Grabern affair, just as those who have taken part in a battle generally do describe it, that is, as they would like it to have been, as they have heard it described by others, and as sounds well, but not at all as it really was. Rostóv was a truthful young man and would on no account have told a deliberate lie. He began his story meaning to tell everything just as it happened, but imperceptibly, involuntarily, and inevitably he lapsed into falsehood. If he had told the truth to his hearers—who like himself had often heard stories of attacks and had formed a definite idea of what an attack was and were expecting to hear just such a story—they would either not have believed him or, still worse, would have thought that Rostóv was himself to blame since what generally happens to the narrators of cavalry attacks had not happened to him. He could not tell them simply that everyone went at a trot and that he fell off his horse and sprained his arm and then ran as hard as he could from a Frenchman into the wood. Besides, to tell everything as it really happened, it would have been necessary to make an effort of will to tell only what happened. It is very difficult to tell the truth, and young people are rarely capable of it. His hearers expected a story of how beside himself and all aflame with excitement, he had flown like a storm at the square, cut his way in, slashed right and left, how his saber had tasted flesh and he had fallen exhausted, and so on. And so he told them all that.

In the middle of his story, just as he was saying: "You cannot imagine what a strange frenzy one experiences during an attack," Prince Andrew, whom Borís was expecting, entered the room. Prince Andrew, who liked to help young men, was flattered by being asked for his assistance and being well disposed toward Borís, who had managed to please him the day before, he wished to do what the young man wanted. Having been sent with papers from Kutúzov to the Tsarévich, he looked in on Borís, hoping to find him alone. When he came in and saw an hussar of the line recounting his military exploits (Prince Andrew could not endure that sort of man), he gave Borís a pleasant smile, frowned as with half-closed eyes he looked at Rostóv, bowed slightly and wearily, and sat down languidly on the sofa: he felt it unpleasant to have dropped in on bad company. Rostóv flushed up on noticing this, but he did not care, this was a mere stranger. Glancing, however, at Borís, he saw that he too seemed ashamed of the hussar of the line.

In spite of Prince Andrew's disagreeable, ironical tone, in spite of the contempt with which Rostóv, from his *fighting* army point of view, regarded all these little adjutants on the staff of whom the newcomer was evidently one, Rostóv felt confused, blushed, and became silent. Borís inquired what news there might be on the staff, and what, without indiscretion, one might ask about our plans.

"We shall probably advance," replied Bolkónski, evidently reluctant to say more in the presence of a stranger.

Berg took the opportunity to ask, with great politeness, whether, as was rumored, the allowance of forage money to captains of companies would be doubled. To this Prince Andrew answered with a smile that he could give no opinion on such an important government order, and Berg laughed gaily.

"As to your business," Prince Andrew continued, addressing Borís, "we will talk of it later" (and he looked round at Rostóv). "Come to me after the review and we will do what is possible."

And, having glanced round the room, Prince Andrew turned to Rostóv, whose state of unconquerable childish embarrassment now changing to anger he did not condescend to notice, and said: "I think you were talking of the Schön Grabern affair? Were you there?"

"I was there," said Rostóv angrily, as if intending to insult the aide-de-camp.

Bolkónski noticed the hussar's state of mind, and it amused him. With a slightly contemptuous smile, he said: "Yes, there are many stories now told about that affair!"

"Yes, stories!" repeated Rostóv loudly, looking with eyes suddenly grown furious, now at Borís, now at Bolkónski. "Yes, many stories! But our stories are the stories of men who have been under the enemy's fire! *Our* stories have some weight, not like the stories of those fellows on the staff who get rewards without doing anything!"

"Of whom you imagine me to be one?" said Prince Andrew, with a quiet and particularly amiable smile.

A strange feeling of exasperation and yet of respect for this man's self-possession mingled at that moment in Rostóv's soul.

"I am not talking about you," he said, "I don't know you and, frankly, I don't want to. I am speaking of the staff in general."

"And I will tell you this," Prince Andrew interrupted in a tone of quiet authority, "you wish to insult me, and I am ready to agree with you that it would be very easy to do so if you haven't sufficient self-respect, but admit that the time and place are very badly chosen. In a day or two we shall all have to take part in a greater and more serious duel, and besides, Drubetskóy, who says he is an old friend of yours, is not at all to blame that my face has the misfortune to displease you. However," he added rising, "you know my name and where to find me, but don't forget that I do not regard either myself or you as having been at all insulted, and as a man older than you, my advice is to let the matter drop. Well then, on Friday after the review I shall expect you, Drubetskóy. *Au revoir!*" exclaimed Prince Andrew, and with a bow to them both he went out.

Only when Prince Andrew was gone did Rostóv think of what he ought to have said. And he was still more angry at having omitted to say it. He ordered his horse at once and, coldly taking leave of Borís, rode home. Should he go to headquarters next day and challenge that affected adjutant, or really let the matter drop, was the question that worried him all the way. He thought angrily of the pleasure he would have at seeing the fright of that small and frail but proud man when covered by his pistol, and then he felt with surprise that of all the men he knew there was none he would so much like to have for a friend as that very adjutant whom he so hated.

CHAPTER VIII

The day after Rostóv had been to see Borís, a review was held of the Austrian and Russian troops, both those freshly arrived from Russia and those who had been campaigning under Kutúzov. The two Emperors, the Russian with his heir the Tsarévich, and the Austrian with the Archduke, inspected the allied army of eighty thousand men.

From early morning the smart clean troops were on the move, forming up on the field before the fortress. Now thousands of feet and bayonets moved and halted at the officers' command, turned with banners flying, formed up at intervals, and wheeled round other similar masses of infantry in different uniforms; now was heard the rhythmic beat of hoofs and the jingling of showy cavalry in blue, red, and green braided uniforms, with smartly dressed bandsmen in front mounted on black, roan, or gray horses; then again, spreading out with the brazen clatter of the polished shining cannon that quivered on the gun carriages and with the smell of linstocks, came the artillery which crawled between the infantry and cavalry and took up its appointed position. Not only the generals in full parade uniforms, with their thin or thick waists drawn in to the utmost, their red necks squeezed into their stiff collars, and wearing scarves and all their decorations, not only the elegant, pomaded officers, but every soldier with his freshly washed and shaven face and his weapons clean and polished to the utmost, and every horse groomed till its coat shone like satin and every hair of its wetted mane lay smooth—felt that no small matter was happening, but an important and solemn affair. Every general and every soldier was conscious of his own insignificance, aware of being but a drop in that ocean of men, and yet at the same time was conscious of his strength as a part of that enormous whole.

From early morning strenuous activities and efforts had begun and by ten o'clock all had been brought into due order. The ranks were drawn up on the vast field. The whole army was extended in three lines: the cavalry in front, behind it the artillery, and behind that again the infantry.

A space like a street was left between each two lines of troops. The three parts of that army were sharply distinguished: Kutúzov's fighting army (with the Pávlograds on the right flank of the front); those recently arrived from Russia, both Guards and regiments of the line; and the Austrian troops. But they all stood in the same lines, under one command, and in a like order.

Like wind over leaves ran an excited whisper: "They're coming! They're coming!" Alarmed voices were heard, and a stir of final preparation swept over all the troops.

From the direction of Olmütz in front of them, a group was seen approaching. And at that moment, though the day was still, a light gust of wind blowing over the army slightly stirred the streamers on the lances and the unfolded standards fluttered against their staffs. It looked as if by that slight motion the army itself was expressing its joy at the approach of the Emperors. One voice was heard shouting: "Eyes front!" Then, like the crowing of cocks at sunrise, this was repeated by others from various sides and all became silent.

In the deathlike stillness only the tramp of horses was heard. This was the Emperors' suites. The Emperors rode up to the flank, and the trumpets of the first cavalry regiment played the general march. It seemed as though not the trumpeters were playing, but as if the army itself, rejoicing at the Emperors' approach, had naturally burst into music. Amid these sounds, only the youthful kindly voice of the Emperor Alexander was clearly heard. He gave the words of greeting, and the first regiment roared "Hurrah!" so deafeningly, continuously, and joyfully that the men themselves were awed by their multitude and the immensity of the power they constituted.

Rostóv, standing in the front lines of Kutúzov's army which the Tsar approached first, experienced the same feeling as every other man in that army: a feeling of self-forgetfulness, a proud consciousness of might, and a passionate attraction to him who was the cause of this triumph.

He felt that at a single word from that man all this vast mass (and he himself an insignificant atom in it) would go through fire and water, commit crime, die, or perform deeds of highest heroism, and so he could not but tremble and his heart stand still at the imminence of that word.

"Hurrah! Hurrah! Hurrah!" thundered from all sides, one regiment after another greeting the Tsar with the strains of the march, and then "Hurrah!"... Then the general march, and again "Hurrah! Hurrah!" growing ever stronger and fuller and merging into a deafening roar.

Till the Tsar reached it, each regiment in its silence and immobility seemed like a lifeless body, but as soon as he came up it became alive, its thunder joining the roar of the whole line along which he had already passed. Through the terrible and deafening roar of those voices, amid the square masses of troops standing motionless as if turned to stone, hundreds of riders composing the suites moved carelessly but symmetrically and above all freely, and in front of them two men—the Emperors. Upon them the undivided, tensely passionate attention of that whole mass of men was concentrated.

The handsome young Emperor Alexander, in the uniform of the Horse Guards, wearing a cocked hat with its peaks front and back, with his pleasant face and resonant though not loud voice, attracted everyone's attention.

Rostóv was not far from the trumpeters, and with his keen sight had recognized the Tsar and watched his approach. When he was within twenty paces, and Nicholas could clearly distinguish every detail of his handsome, happy young face, he experienced a feeling of tenderness and ecstasy such as he had never before known. Every trait and every movement of the Tsar's seemed to him enchanting.

Stopping in front of the Pávlograds, the Tsar said something in French to the Austrian Emperor and smiled.

Seeing that smile, Rostóv involuntarily smiled himself and felt a still stronger flow of love for his sovereign. He longed to show that love in some way and knowing that this was impossible was ready to cry. The Tsar called the colonel of the regiment and said a few words to him.

"Oh God, what would happen to me if the Emperor spoke to me?" thought Rostóv. "I should die of happiness!"

The Tsar addressed the officers also: "I thank you all, gentlemen, I thank you with my whole heart." To Rostóv every word sounded like a voice from heaven. How gladly would he have died at once for his Tsar!

"You have earned the St. George's standards and will be worthy of them."

"Oh, to die, to die for him," thought Rostóv.

The Tsar said something more which Rostóv did not hear, and the soldiers, straining their lungs, shouted "Hurrah!"

Rostóv too, bending over his saddle, shouted "Hurrah!" with all his might, feeling that he would like to injure himself by that shout, if only to express his rapture fully.

The Tsar stopped a few minutes in front of the hussars as if undecided.

"How can the Emperor be undecided?" thought Rostóv, but then even this indecision appeared to him majestic and enchanting, like everything else the Tsar did.

That hesitation lasted only an instant. The Tsar's foot, in the narrow pointed boot then fashionable, touched the groin of the bobtailed bay mare he rode, his hand in a white glove gathered up the reins, and he moved off accompanied by an irregularly swaying sea of aides-de-camp. Farther and farther he rode away, stopping at other regiments, till at last only his white plumes were visible to Rostóv from amid the suites that surrounded the Emperors.

Among the gentlemen of the suite, Rostóv noticed Bolkónski, sitting his horse indolently and carelessly. Rostóv recalled their quarrel of yesterday and the question presented itself whether he ought or ought not to challenge Bolkónski. "Of course not!" he now thought. "Is it worth thinking or speaking of it at such a moment? At a time of such love, such rapture, and such self-sacrifice, what do any of our quarrels and affronts matter? I love and forgive everybody now."

When the Emperor had passed nearly all the regiments, the troops began a ceremonial march past him, and Rostóv on Bedouin, recently purchased from Denísov, rode past too, at the rear of his squadron—that is, alone and in full view of the Emperor.

Before he reached him, Rostóv, who was a splendid horseman, spurred Bedouin twice and successfully put him to the showy trot in which the animal went when excited. Bending his foaming muzzle to his chest, his tail extended, Bedouin, as if also conscious of the Emperor's eye upon him, passed splendidly, lifting his feet with a high and graceful action, as if flying through the air without touching the ground.

Rostóv himself, his legs well back and his stomach drawn in and feeling himself one with his horse, rode past the Emperor with a frowning but blissful face "like a vewy devil," as Denísov expressed it.

"Fine fellows, the Pávlograds!" remarked the Emperor.

"My God, how happy I should be if he ordered me to leap into the fire this instant!" thought Rostóv.

When the review was over, the newly arrived officers, and also Kutúzov's, collected in groups and began to talk about the awards, about the Austrians and their uniforms, about their lines, about Bonaparte, and how badly the latter would fare now, especially if the Essen corps arrived and Prussia took our side.

But the talk in every group was chiefly about the Emperor Alexander. His every word and movement was described with ecstasy.

They all had but one wish: to advance as soon as possible against the enemy under the Emperor's command. Commanded by the Emperor himself they could not fail to vanquish anyone, be it whom it might: so thought Rostóv and most of the officers after the review.

All were then more confident of victory than the winning of two battles would have made them.

CHAPTER IX

The day after the review, Borís, in his best uniform and with his comrade Berg's best wishes for success, rode to Olmütz to see Bolkónski, wishing to profit by his friendliness and obtain for himself the best post he could—preferably that of adjutant to some important personage, a position in the army which seemed to him most attractive. "It is all very well for Rostóv, whose father sends him ten thousand rubles at a time, to talk about not wishing to cringe to anybody and not be anyone's lackey, but I who have nothing but my brains have to make a career and must not miss opportunities, but must avail myself of them!" he reflected.

He did not find Prince Andrew in Olmütz that day, but the appearance of the town where the headquarters and the diplomatic corps were stationed and the two Emperors were living with their suites, households, and courts only strengthened his desire to belong to that higher world.

He knew no one, and despite his smart Guardsman's uniform, all these exalted personages passing in the streets in their elegant carriages with their plumes, ribbons, and medals, both courtiers and military men, seemed so immeasurably above him, an insignificant officer of the Guards, that they not only did not wish to, but simply could not, be aware of his existence. At the quarters of the commander in chief, Kutúzov, where he inquired for Bolkónski, all the adjutants and even the orderlies looked at him as if they wished to impress on him that a great many officers like him were always coming there and that everybody was heartily sick of them. In spite of this, or rather because of it, next day, November 15, after dinner he again went to Olmütz and, entering the house occupied by Kutúzov, asked for Bolkónski. Prince Andrew was in and Borís was shown into a large hall probably formerly used for dancing, but in which five beds now stood, and furniture of various kinds: a table, chairs, and a clavichord. One adjutant, nearest the door, was sitting at the table in a Persian dressing gown, writing. Another, the red, stout Nesvítski, lay on a bed with his arms under his head, laughing with an officer who had sat down beside him. A third was playing a Viennese waltz on the clavichord, while a fourth, lying on the clavichord, sang the tune. Bolkónski was not there. None of these gentlemen changed his position on seeing Borís. The one who was writing and whom Borís addressed turned round crossly and told him Bolkónski was on duty and that he should go through the door on the left into the reception room if he wished to see him. Borís thanked him and went to the reception room, where he found some ten officers and generals.

When he entered, Prince Andrew, his eyes drooping contemptuously (with that peculiar expression of polite weariness which plainly says, "If it were not my duty I would not talk to you for a moment"), was listening to an old Russian general with decorations, who stood very erect, almost on tiptoe, with a soldier's obsequious expression on his purple face, reporting something.

"Very well, then, be so good as to wait," said Prince Andrew to the general, in Russian, speaking with the French intonation he affected when he wished to speak contemptuously, and noticing Borís, Prince Andrew, paying no more heed to the general who ran after him imploring him to hear something more, nodded and turned to him with a cheerful smile.

At that moment Borís clearly realized what he had before surmised, that in the army, besides the subordination and discipline prescribed in the military code, which he and the others knew in the regiment, there was another, more important, subordination, which made this tight-laced, purple-faced general wait respectfully while Captain Prince Andrew, for his own pleasure, chose to chat with Lieutenant Drubetskóy. More than ever was Borís resolved to serve in future not according to the written code, but under this unwritten law. He felt now that merely by having been recommended to Prince Andrew he had already risen above the general who at the front had the power to annihilate him, a lieutenant of the Guards. Prince Andrew came up to him and took his hand.

"I am very sorry you did not find me in yesterday. I was fussing about with Germans all day. We went with Weyrother to survey the dispositions. When Germans start being accurate, there's no end to it!"

Borís smiled, as if he understood what Prince Andrew was alluding to as something generally known. But it was the first time he had heard Weyrother's name, or even the term "dispositions."

"Well, my dear fellow, so you still want to be an adjutant? I have been thinking about you."

"Yes, I was thinking"—for some reason Borís could not help blushing—"of asking the commander in chief. He has had a letter from Prince Kurágin about me. I only wanted to ask because I fear the Guards won't be in action," he added as if in apology.

"All right, all right. We'll talk it over," replied Prince Andrew. "Only let me report this gentleman's business, and I shall be at your disposal."

While Prince Andrew went to report about the purple-faced general, that gentleman—evidently not sharing Borís' conception of the advantages of the unwritten code of subordination—looked so fixedly at the presumptuous lieutenant who had prevented his finishing what he had to say to the adjutant that Borís felt uncomfortable. He turned away and waited impatiently for Prince Andrew's return from the commander in chief's room.

"You see, my dear fellow, I have been thinking about you," said Prince Andrew when they had gone into the large room where the clavichord was. "It's no use your going to the commander in chief. He would say a lot of pleasant things, ask you to dinner" ("That would not be bad as regards the unwritten code," thought Borís), "but nothing more would come of it. There will soon be a battalion of us aides-de-camp and adjutants! But this is what we'll do: I have a good friend, an adjutant general and an excellent fellow, Prince Dolgorúkov; and though you may not know it, the fact is that now Kutúzov with his staff and all of us count for nothing. Everything is now centered round the Emperor. So we will go to Dolgorúkov; I have to go there anyhow and I have already spoken to him about you. We shall see whether he cannot attach you to himself or find a place for you somewhere nearer the sun."

Prince Andrew always became specially keen when he had to guide a young man and help him to worldly success. Under cover of obtaining help of this kind for another, which from pride he would never accept for himself, he kept in touch with the circle which confers success and which attracted him. He very readily took up Borís' cause and went with him to Dolgorúkov.

It was late in the evening when they entered the palace at Olmütz occupied by the Emperors and their retinues.

That same day a council of war had been held in which all the members of the Hofkriegsrath and both Emperors took part. At that council, contrary to the views of the old generals Kutúzov and Prince Schwartzenberg, it had been decided to advance immediately and give battle to Bonaparte. The council of war was just over when Prince Andrew accompanied by Borís arrived at the palace to find Dolgorúkov. Everyone at headquarters was still under the spell of the day's council, at which the party of the young had triumphed. The voices of those who counseled delay and advised waiting for something else before advancing had been so completely silenced and their arguments confuted by such conclusive evidence of the advantages of attacking that what had been discussed at the council—the coming battle and the victory that would certainly result from it—no longer seemed to be in the future but in the past. All the advantages were on our side. Our enormous forces, undoubtedly superior to Napoleon's, were concentrated in one place, the troops inspired by the Emperors' presence were eager for action. The strategic position where the operations would take place was familiar in all its details to the Austrian General Weyrother: a lucky accident had ordained that the Austrian army should maneuver the previous year on the very fields where the French had now to be fought; the adjacent locality was known and shown in every detail on the maps, and Bonaparte, evidently weakened, was undertaking nothing.

Dolgorúkov, one of the warmest advocates of an attack, had just returned from the council, tired and exhausted but eager and proud of the victory that had been gained. Prince Andrew introduced his protégé, but Prince Dolgorúkov politely and firmly pressing his hand said nothing to Borís and, evidently unable to suppress the thoughts which were uppermost in his mind at that moment, addressed Prince Andrew in French.

"Ah, my dear fellow, what a battle we have gained! God grant that the one that will result from it will be as victorious! However, dear fellow," he said abruptly and eagerly, "I must confess to having been unjust to the Austrians and especially to Weyrother. What exactitude, what minuteness, what knowledge of the locality, what foresight for every eventuality, every possibility even to the smallest detail! No, my dear fellow, no conditions better than our present ones could have been devised. This combination of Austrian precision with Russian valor—what more could be wished for?"

"So the attack is definitely resolved on?" asked Bolkónski.

"And do you know, my dear fellow, it seems to me that Bonaparte has decidedly lost bearings, you know that a letter was received from him today for the Emperor." Dolgorúkov smiled significantly.

"Is that so? And what did he say?" inquired Bolkónski.

"What can he say? Tra-di-ri-di-ra and so on... merely to gain time. I tell you he is in our hands, that's certain! But what was most amusing," he continued, with a sudden, good-natured laugh, "was that we could not think how to address the reply! If not as 'Consul' and of course not as 'Emperor,' it seemed to me it should be to 'General Bonaparte.'"

"But between not recognizing him as Emperor and calling him General Bonaparte, there is a difference," remarked Bolkónski.

"That's just it," interrupted Dolgorúkov quickly, laughing. "You know Bilíbin—he's a very clever fellow. He suggested addressing him as 'Usurper and Enemy of Mankind.'"

Dolgorúkov laughed merrily.

"Only that?" said Bolkónski.

"All the same, it was Bilíbin who found a suitable form for the address. He is a wise and clever fellow."

"What was it?"

"'To the Head of the French Government... *Au chef du gouvernementfrançais*,'" said Dolgorúkov, with grave satisfaction. "Good, wasn't it?"

"Yes, but he will dislike it extremely," said Bolkónski.

"Oh yes, very much! My brother knows him, he's dined with him—the present Emperor—more than once in Paris, and tells me he never met a more cunning or subtle diplomatist—you know, a combination of French adroitness and Italian play-acting! Do you know the tale about him and Count Markóv? Count Markóv was the only man who knew how to handle him. You know the story of the handkerchief? It is delightful!"

And the talkative Dolgorúkov, turning now to Borís, now to Prince Andrew, told how Bonaparte wishing to test Markóv, our ambassador, purposely dropped a handkerchief in front of him and stood looking at Markóv, probably expecting Markóv to pick it up for him, and how Markóv immediately dropped his own beside it and picked it up without touching Bonaparte's.

"Delightful!" said Bolkónski. "But I have come to you, Prince, as a petitioner on behalf of this young man. You see..." but before Prince Andrew could finish, an aide-de-camp came in to summon Dolgorúkov to the Emperor.

"Oh, what a nuisance," said Dolgorúkov, getting up hurriedly and pressing the hands of Prince Andrew and Borís. "You know I should be very glad to do all in my power both for you and for this dear young man." Again he pressed the hand of the latter with an expression of good-natured, sincere, and animated levity. "But you see... another time!"

Borís was excited by the thought of being so close to the higher powers as he felt himself to be at that moment. He was conscious that here he was in contact with the springs that set in motion the enormous movements of the mass of which in his regiment he felt himself a tiny, obedient, and insignificant atom. They followed Prince Dolgorúkov out into the corridor and met—coming out of the door of the Emperor's room by which Dolgorúkov had entered—a short man in civilian clothes with a clever face and sharply projecting jaw which, without spoiling his face, gave him a peculiar vivacity and shiftiness of expression. This short man nodded to Dolgorúkov as to an intimate friend and stared at Prince Andrew with cool intensity, walking straight toward him and evidently expecting him to bow or to step out of his way. Prince Andrew did neither: a look of animosity appeared on his face and the other turned away and went down the side of the corridor.

"Who was that?" asked Borís.

"He is one of the most remarkable, but to me most unpleasant of men—the Minister of Foreign Affairs, Prince Adam Czartoryski.... It is such men as he who decide the fate of nations," added Bolkónski with a sigh he could not suppress, as they passed out of the palace.

Next day, the army began its campaign, and up to the very battle of Austerlitz, Borís was unable to see either Prince Andrew or Dolgorúkov again and remained for a while with the Ismáylov regiment.

CHAPTER X

At dawn on the sixteenth of November, Denísov's squadron, in which Nicholas Rostóv served and which was in Prince Bagratión's detachment, moved from the place where it had spent the night, advancing into action as arranged, and after going behind other columns for about two thirds of a mile was stopped on the highroad. Rostóv saw the Cossacks and then the first and second squadrons of hussars and infantry battalions and artillery pass by and go forward and then Generals Bagratión and Dolgorúkov ride past with their adjutants. All the fear before action which he had experienced as previously, all the inner struggle to conquer that fear, all his dreams of distinguishing himself as a true hussar in this battle, had been wasted. Their squadron remained in reserve and Nicholas Rostóv spent that day in a dull and wretched mood. At nine in the morning, he heard firing in front and shouts of *hurrah*, and saw wounded being brought back (there were not many of them), and at last he saw how a whole detachment of French cavalry was brought in, convoyed by a *sótnya* of Cossacks. Evidently the affair was over and, though not big, had been a successful engagement. The men and officers returning spoke of a brilliant victory, of the occupation of the town of Wischau and the capture of a whole French squadron. The day was bright and sunny after a sharp night frost, and the cheerful glitter of that autumn day was in keeping with the news of victory which was conveyed, not only by the tales of those who had taken part in it, but also by the joyful expression on the faces of soldiers, officers, generals, and adjutants, as they passed Rostóv going or coming. And Nicholas, who had vainly suffered all the dread that precedes a battle and had spent that happy day in inactivity, was all the more depressed.

"Come here, Wostóv. Let's dwink to dwown our gwief!" shouted Denísov, who had settled down by the roadside with a flask and some food.

The officers gathered round Denísov's canteen, eating and talking.

"There! They are bringing another!" cried one of the officers, indicating a captive French dragoon who was being brought in on foot by two Cossacks.

One of them was leading by the bridle a fine large French horse he had taken from the prisoner.

"Sell us that horse!" Denísov called out to the Cossacks.

"If you like, your honor!"

The officers got up and stood round the Cossacks and their prisoner. The French dragoon was a young Alsatian who spoke French with a German accent. He was breathless with agitation, his face was red, and when he heard some French spoken he at once began speaking to the officers, addressing first one, then another. He said he would not have been taken, it was not his fault but the corporal's who had sent him to seize some horsecloths, though he had told him the Russians were there. And at every word he added: "But don't hurt my little horse!" and stroked the animal. It was plain that he did not quite grasp where he was. Now he excused himself for having been taken prisoner and now, imagining himself before his own officers, insisted on his soldierly discipline and zeal in the service. He brought with him into our rearguard all the freshness of atmosphere of the French army, which was so alien to us.

The Cossacks sold the horse for two gold pieces, and Rostóv, being the richest of the officers now that he had received his money, bought it.

"But don't hurt my little horse!" said the Alsatian good-naturedly to Rostóv when the animal was handed over to the hussar.

Rostóv smilingly reassured the dragoon and gave him money.

"Alley! Alley!" said the Cossack, touching the prisoner's arm to make him go on.

"The Emperor! The Emperor!" was suddenly heard among the hussars.

All began to run and bustle, and Rostóv saw coming up the road behind him several riders with white plumes in their hats. In a moment everyone was in his place, waiting.

Rostóv did not know or remember how he ran to his place and mounted. Instantly his regret at not having been in action and his dejected mood amid people of whom he was weary had gone, instantly every thought of himself had vanished. He was filled with happiness at his nearness to the Emperor. He felt that this nearness by itself made up to him for the day he had lost. He was happy as a lover when the longed-for moment of meeting arrives. Not daring to look round and without looking round, he was ecstatically conscious of *his* approach. He felt it not only from the sound of the hoofs of the approaching cavalcade, but because as *he* drew near everything grew brighter, more joyful, more significant, and more festive around him. Nearer and nearer to Rostóv came that sun shedding beams of mild and majestic light around, and already he felt himself enveloped in those beams, he heard *his* voice, that kindly, calm, and majestic voice that was yet so simple! And as if in accord with Rostóv's feeling, there was a deathly stillness amid which was heard the Emperor's voice.

"The Pávlograd hussars?" he inquired.

"The reserves, sire!" replied a voice, a very human one compared to that which had said: "The Pávlograd hussars?"

The Emperor drew level with Rostóv and halted. Alexander's face was even more beautiful than it had been three days before at the review. It shone with such gaiety and youth, such innocent youth, that it suggested the liveliness of a fourteen-year-old boy, and yet it was the face of the majestic Emperor. Casually, while surveying the squadron, the Emperor's eyes met Rostóv's and rested on them for not more than two seconds. Whether or no the Emperor understood what was going on in Rostóv's soul (it seemed to Rostóv that he understood everything), at any rate his light-blue eyes gazed for about two seconds into Rostóv's face. A gentle, mild light poured from them. Then all at once he raised his eyebrows, abruptly touched his horse with his left foot, and galloped on.

The younger Emperor could not restrain his wish to be present at the battle and, in spite of the remonstrances of his courtiers, at twelve o'clock left the third column with which he had been and galloped toward the vanguard. Before he came up with the hussars, several adjutants met him with news of the successful result of the action.

This battle, which consisted in the capture of a French squadron, was represented as a brilliant victory over the French, and so the Emperor and the whole army, especially while the smoke hung over the battlefield, believed that the French had been defeated and were retreating against their will. A few minutes after the Emperor had passed, the Pávlograd division was ordered to advance. In Wischau itself, a petty German town, Rostóv saw the Emperor again. In the market place, where there had been some rather heavy firing before the Emperor's arrival, lay several killed and wounded soldiers whom there had not been time to move. The Emperor, surrounded by his suite of officers and courtiers, was riding a bobtailed chestnut mare, a different one from that which he had ridden at the review, and bending to one side he gracefully held a gold lorgnette to his eyes and looked at a soldier who lay prone, with blood on his uncovered head. The wounded soldier was so dirty, coarse, and revolting that his proximity to the Emperor shocked Rostóv. Rostóv saw how the Emperor's rather round shoulders shuddered as if a cold shiver had run down them, how his left foot began convulsively tapping the horse's side with the spur, and how the well-trained horse looked round unconcerned and did not stir. An adjutant, dismounting, lifted the soldier under the arms to place him on a stretcher that had been brought. The soldier groaned.

"Gently, gently! Can't you do it more gently?" said the Emperor apparently suffering more than the dying soldier, and he rode away.

Rostóv saw tears filling the Emperor's eyes and heard him, as he was riding away, say to Czartoryski: "What a terrible thing war is: what a terrible thing! *Quelle terrible chose que la guerre!*"

The troops of the vanguard were stationed before Wischau, within sight of the enemy's lines, which all day long had yielded ground to us at the least firing. The Emperor's gratitude was announced to the vanguard, rewards were promised, and the men received a double ration of vodka. The campfires crackled and the soldiers' songs resounded even more merrily than on the previous night. Denísov celebrated his promotion to the rank of major, and Rostóv, who had already drunk enough, at the end of the feast proposed the Emperor's health. "Not 'our Sovereign, the Emperor,' as they say at official dinners," said he, "but the health of our Sovereign, that good, enchanting, and great man! Let us drink to his health and to the certain defeat of the French!"

"If we fought before," he said, "not letting the French pass, as at Schön Grabern, what shall we not do now when *he* is at the front? We will all die for him gladly! Is it not so, gentlemen? Perhaps I am not saying it right, I have drunk a good deal—but that is how I feel, and so do you too! To the health of Alexander the First! Hurrah!"

"Hurrah!" rang the enthusiastic voices of the officers.

And the old cavalry captain, Kírsten, shouted enthusiastically and no less sincerely than the twenty-year-old Rostóv.

When the officers had emptied and smashed their glasses, Kírsten filled others and, in shirt sleeves and breeches, went glass in hand to the soldiers' bonfires and with his long graymustache, his white chest showing under his open shirt, he stood in a majestic pose in the light of the campfire, waving his uplifted arm.

"Lads! here's to our Sovereign, the Emperor, and victory over our enemies! Hurrah!" he exclaimed in his dashing, old, hussar's baritone.

The hussars crowded round and responded heartily with loud shouts.

Late that night, when all had separated, Denísov with his short hand patted his favorite, Rostóv, on the shoulder.

"As there's no one to fall in love with on campaign, he's fallen in love with the Tsar," he said.

"Denísov, don't make fun of it!" cried Rostóv. "It is such a lofty, beautiful feeling, such a..."

"I believe it, I believe it, fwiend, and I share and appwove..."

"No, you don't understand!"

And Rostóv got up and went wandering among the campfires, dreaming of what happiness it would be to die—not in saving the Emperor's life (he did not even dare to dream of that), but simply to die before his eyes. He really was in love with the Tsar and the glory of the Russian arms and the hope of future triumph. And he was not the only man to experience that feeling during those memorable days preceding the battle of Austerlitz: nine tenths of the men in the Russian army were then in love, though less ecstatically, with their Tsar and the glory of the Russian arms.

CHAPTER XI

The next day the Emperor stopped at Wischau, and Villier, his physician, was repeatedly summoned to see him. At headquarters and among the troops near by the news spread that the Emperor was unwell. He ate nothing and had slept badly that night, those around him reported. The cause of this indisposition was the strong impression made on his sensitive mind by the sight of the killed and wounded.

At daybreak on the seventeenth, a French officer who had come with a flag of truce, demanding an audience with the Russian Emperor, was brought into Wischau from our outposts. This officer was Savary. The Emperor had only just fallen asleep and so Savary had to wait. At midday he was admitted to the Emperor, and an hour later he rode off with Prince Dolgorúkov to the advanced post of the French army.

It was rumored that Savary had been sent to propose to Alexander a meeting with Napoleon. To the joy and pride of the whole army, a personal interview was refused, and instead of the Sovereign, Prince Dolgorúkov, the victor at Wischau, was sent with Savary to negotiate with Napoleon if, contrary to expectations, these negotiations were actuated by a real desire for peace.

Toward evening Dolgorúkov came back, went straight to the Tsar, and remained alone with him for a long time.

On the eighteenth and nineteenth of November, the army advanced two days' march and the enemy's outposts after a brief interchange of shots retreated. In the highest army circles from midday on the nineteenth, a great, excitedly bustling activity began which lasted till the morning of the twentieth, when the memorable battle of Austerlitz was fought.

Till midday on the nineteenth, the activity—the eager talk, running to and fro, and dispatching of adjutants—was confined to the Emperor's headquarters. But on the afternoon of that day, this activity reached Kutúzov's headquarters and the staffs of the commanders of columns. By evening, the adjutants had spread it to all ends and parts of the army, and in the night from the nineteenth to the twentieth, the whole eighty thousand allied troops rose from their bivouacs to the hum of voices, and the army swayed and started in one enormous mass six miles long.

The concentrated activity which had begun at the Emperor's headquarters in the morning and had started the whole movement that followed was like the first movement of the main wheel of a large tower clock. One wheel slowly moved, another was set in motion, and a third, and wheels began to revolve faster and faster, levers and cogwheels to work, chimes to play, figures to pop out, and the hands to advance with regular motion as a result of all that activity.

Just as in the mechanism of a clock, so in the mechanism of the military machine, an impulse once given leads to the final result; and just as indifferently quiescent till the moment when motion is transmitted to them are the parts of the mechanism which the impulse has not yet reached. Wheels creak on their axles as the cogs engage one another and the revolving pulleys whirr with the rapidity of their movement, but a neighboring wheel is as quiet and motionless as though it were prepared to remain so for a hundred years; but the moment comes when the lever catches it and obeying the impulse that wheel begins to creak and joins in the common motion the result and aim of which are beyond its ken.

Just as in a clock, the result of the complicated motion of innumerable wheels and pulleys is merely a slow and regular movement of the hands which show the time, so the result of all the complicated human activities of 160,000 Russians and French—all their passions, desires, remorse, humiliations, sufferings, outbursts of pride, fear, and enthusiasm—was only the loss of the battle of Austerlitz, the so-called battle of the three Emperors—that is to say, a slow movement of the hand on the dial of human history.

Prince Andrew was on duty that day and in constant attendance on the commander in chief.

At six in the evening, Kutúzov went to the Emperor's headquarters and after staying but a short time with the Tsar went to see the grand marshal of the court, Count Tolstóy.

Bolkónski took the opportunity to go in to get some details of the coming action from Dolgorúkov. He felt that Kutúzov was upset and dissatisfied about something and that at headquarters they were dissatisfied with him, and also that at the Emperor's headquarters everyone adopted toward him the tone of men who know something others do not know: he therefore wished to speak to Dolgorúkov.

"Well, how d'you do, my dear fellow?" said Dolgorúkov, who was sitting at tea with Bilíbin. "The fete is for tomorrow. How is your old fellow? Out of sorts?"

"I won't say he is out of sorts, but I fancy he would like to be heard."

"But they heard him at the council of war and will hear him when he talks sense, but to temporize and wait for something now when Bonaparte fears nothing so much as a general battle is impossible."

"Yes, you have seen him?" said Prince Andrew. "Well, what is Bonaparte like? How did he impress you?"

"Yes, I saw him, and am convinced that he fears nothing so much as a general engagement," repeated Dolgorúkov, evidently prizing this general conclusion which he had arrived at from his interview with Napoleon. "If he weren't afraid of a battle why did he ask for that interview? Why negotiate, and above all why retreat, when to retreat is so contrary to his method of conducting war? Believe me, he is afraid, afraid of a general battle. His hour has come! Mark my words!"

"But tell me, what is he like, eh?" said Prince Andrew again.

"He is a man in a gray overcoat, very anxious that I should call him 'Your Majesty,' but who, to his chagrin, got no title from me! That's the sort of man he is, and nothing more," replied Dolgorúkov, looking round at Bilíbin with a smile.

"Despite my great respect for old Kutúzov," he continued, "we should be a nice set of fellows if we were to wait about and so give him a chance to escape, or to trick us, now that we certainly have him in our hands! No, we mustn't forget Suvórov and his rule—not to put yourself in a position to be attacked, but yourself to attack. Believe me in war the energy of young men often shows the way better than all the experience of old Cunctators."

"But in what position are we going to attack him? I have been at the outposts today and it is impossible to say where his chief forces are situated," said Prince Andrew.

He wished to explain to Dolgorúkov a plan of attack he had himself formed.

"Oh, that is all the same," Dolgorúkov said quickly, and getting up he spread a map on the table. "All eventualities have been foreseen. If he is standing before Brünn..."

And Prince Dolgorúkov rapidly but indistinctly explained Weyrother's plan of a flanking movement.

Prince Andrew began to reply and to state his own plan, which might have been as good as Weyrother's, but for the disadvantage that Weyrother's had already been approved. As soon as Prince Andrew began to demonstrate the defects of the latter and the merits of his own plan, Prince Dolgorúkov ceased to listen to him and gazed absent-mindedly not at the map, but at Prince Andrew's face.

"There will be a council of war at Kutúzov's tonight, though; you can say all this there," remarked Dolgorúkov.

"I will do so," said Prince Andrew, moving away from the map.

"Whatever are you bothering about, gentlemen?" said Bilíbin, who, till then, had listened with an amused smile to their conversation and now was evidently ready with a joke. "Whether tomorrow brings victory or defeat, the glory of our Russian arms is secure. Except your Kutúzov, there is not a single Russian in command of a column! The commanders are: Herr General Wimpfen, le Comte de Langeron, le Prince de Lichtenstein, le Prince de Hohenlohe, and finally Prishprish, and so on like all those Polish names."

"Be quiet, backbiter!" said Dolgorúkov. "It is not true; there are now two Russians, Milorádovich, and Dokhtúrov, and there would be a third, Count Arakchéev, if his nerves were not too weak."

"However, I think General Kutúzov has come out," said Prince Andrew. "I wish you good luck and success, gentlemen!" he added and went out after shaking hands with Dolgorúkov and Bilíbin.

On the way home, Prince Andrew could not refrain from asking Kutúzov, who was sitting silently beside him, what he thought of tomorrow's battle.

Kutúzov looked sternly at his adjutant and, after a pause, replied: "I think the battle will be lost, and so I told Count Tolstóy and asked him to tell the Emperor. What do you think he replied? 'But, my dear general, I am engaged with rice and cutlets, look after military matters yourself!' Yes... That was the answer I got!"

CHAPTER XII

Shortly after nine o'clock that evening, Weyrother drove with his plans to Kutúzov's quarters where the council of war was to be held. All the commanders of columns were summoned to the commander in chief's and with the exception of Prince Bagratión, who declined to come, were all there at the appointed time.

Weyrother, who was in full control of the proposed battle, by his eagerness and briskness presented a marked contrast to the dissatisfied and drowsy Kutúzov, who reluctantly played the part of chairman and president of the council of war. Weyrother evidently felt himself to be at the head of a movement that had already become unrestrainable. He was like a horse running downhill harnessed to a heavy cart. Whether he was pulling it or being pushed by it he did not know, but rushed along at headlong speed with no time to consider what this movement might lead to. Weyrother had been twice that evening to the enemy's picket line to reconnoiter personally, and twice to the Emperors, Russian and Austrian, to report and explain, and to his headquarters where he had dictated the dispositions in German, and now, much exhausted, he arrived at Kutúzov's.

He was evidently so busy that he even forgot to be polite to the commander in chief. He interrupted him, talked rapidly and indistinctly, without looking at the man he was addressing, and did not reply to questions put to him. He was bespattered with mud and had a pitiful, weary, and distracted air, though at the same time he was haughty and self-confident.

Kutúzov was occupying a nobleman's castle of modest dimensions near Ostralitz. In the large drawing room which had become the commander in chief's office were gathered Kutúzov himself, Weyrother, and the members of the council of war. They were drinking tea, and only awaited Prince Bagratión to begin the council. At last Bagratión's orderly came with the news that the prince could not attend. Prince Andrew came in to inform the commander in chief of this and, availing himself of permission previously given him by Kutúzov to be present at the council, he remained in the room.

"Since Prince Bagratión is not coming, we may begin," said Weyrother, hurriedly rising from his seat and going up to the table on which an enormous map of the environs of Brünn was spread out.

Kutúzov, with his uniform unbuttoned so that his fat neck bulged over his collar as if escaping, was sitting almost asleep in a low chair, with his podgy old hands resting symmetrically on its arms. At the sound of Weyrother's voice, he opened his one eye with an effort.

"Yes, yes, if you please! It is already late," said he, and nodding his head he let it droop and again closed his eye.

If at first the members of the council thought that Kutúzov was pretending to sleep, the sounds his nose emitted during the reading that followed proved that the commander in chief at that moment was absorbed by a far more serious matter than a desire to show his contempt for the dispositions or anything else—he was engaged in satisfying the irresistible human need for sleep. He really was asleep. Weyrother, with the gesture of a man too busy to lose a moment, glanced at Kutúzov and, having convinced himself that he was asleep, took up a paper and in a loud, monotonous voice began to read out the dispositions for the impending battle, under a heading which he also read out:

"Dispositions for an attack on the enemy position behind Kobelnitz and Sokolnitz, November 30, 1805."

The dispositions were very complicated and difficult. They began as follows:

"As the enemy's left wing rests on wooded hills and his right extends along Kobelnitz and Sokolnitz behind the ponds that are there, while we, on the other hand, with our left wing by far outflank his right, it is advantageous to attack the enemy's latter wing especially if we occupy the villages of Sokolnitz and Kobelnitz, whereby we can both fall on his flank and pursue him over the plain between Schlappanitz and the Thuerassa forest, avoiding the defiles of Schlappanitz and Bellowitz which cover the enemy's front. For this object it is necessary that... The first column marches... The second column marches... The third column marches..." and so on, read Weyrother.

The generals seemed to listen reluctantly to the difficult dispositions. The tall, fair-haired General Buxhöwden stood, leaning his back against the wall, his eyes fixed on a burning candle, and seemed not to listen or even to wish to be thought to listen. Exactly opposite Weyrother, with his glistening wide-open eyes fixed upon him and his mustache twisted upwards, sat the ruddy Milorádovich in a military pose, his elbows turned outwards, his hands on his knees, and his shoulders raised. He remained stubbornly silent, gazing at Weyrother's face, and only turned away his eyes when the Austrian chief of staff finished reading. Then Milorádovich looked round significantly at the other generals. But one could not tell from that significant look whether he agreed or disagreed and was satisfied or not with the arrangements. Next to Weyrother sat Count Langeron who, with a subtle smile that never left his typically southern French face during the whole time of the reading, gazed at his delicate fingers which rapidly twirled by its corners a gold snuffbox on which was a portrait. In the middle of one of the longest sentences, he stopped the rotary motion of the snuffbox, raised his head, and with inimical politeness lurking in the corners of his thin lips interrupted Weyrother, wishing to say something. But the Austrian general, continuing to read, frowned angrily and jerked his elbows, as if to say: "You can tell me your views later, but now be so good as to look at the map and listen." Langeron lifted his eyes with an expression of perplexity, turned round to Milorádovich as if seeking an explanation, but meeting the latter's impressive but meaningless gaze drooped his eyes sadly and again took to twirling his snuffbox.

"A geography lesson!" he muttered as if to himself, but loud enough to be heard.

Przebyszéwski, with respectful but dignified politeness, held his hand to his ear toward Weyrother, with the air of a man absorbed in attention. Dohktúrov, a little man, sat opposite Weyrother, with an assiduous and modest mien, and stooping over the outspread map conscientiously studied the dispositions and the unfamiliar locality. He asked Weyrother several times to repeat words he had not clearly heard and the difficult names of villages. Weyrother complied and Dohktúrov noted them down.

When the reading which lasted more than an hour was over, Langeron again brought his snuffbox to rest and, without looking at Weyrother or at anyone in particular, began to say how difficult it was to carry out such a plan in which the enemy's position was assumed to be known, whereas it was perhaps not known, since the enemy was in movement. Langeron's objections were valid but it was obvious that their chief aim was to show General Weyrother—who had read his dispositions with as much self-confidence as if he were addressing school children—that he had to do, not with fools, but with men who could teach him something in military matters.

When the monotonous sound of Weyrother's voice ceased, Kutúzov opened his eye as a miller wakes up when the soporific drone of the mill wheel is interrupted. He listened to what Langeron said, as if remarking, "So you are still at that silly business!" quickly closed his eye again, and let his head sink still lower.

Langeron, trying as virulently as possible to sting Weyrother's vanity as author of the military plan, argued that Bonaparte might easily attack instead of being attacked, and so render the whole of this plan perfectly worthless. Weyrother met all objections with a firm and contemptuous smile, evidently prepared beforehand to meet all objections be they what they might.

"If he could attack us, he would have done so today," said he.

"So you think he is powerless?" said Langeron.

"He has forty thousand men at most," replied Weyrother, with the smile of a doctor to whom an old wife wishes to explain the treatment of a case.

"In that case he is inviting his doom by awaiting our attack," said Langeron, with a subtly ironical smile, again glancing round for support to Milorádovich who was near him.

But Milorádovich was at that moment evidently thinking of anything rather than of what the generals were disputing about.

"*Ma foi!*" said he, "tomorrow we shall see all that on the battlefield."

Weyrother again gave that smile which seemed to say that to him it was strange and ridiculous to meet objections from Russian generals and to have to prove to them what he had not merely convinced himself of, but had also convinced the sovereign Emperors of.

"The enemy has quenched his fires and a continual noise is heard from his camp," said he. "What does that mean? Either he is retreating, which is the only thing we need fear, or he is changing his position." (He smiled ironically.) "But even if he also took up a position in the Thuerassa, he merely saves us a great deal of trouble and all our arrangements to the minutest detail remain the same."

"How is that?..." began Prince Andrew, who had for long been waiting an opportunity to express his doubts.

Kutúzov here woke up, coughed heavily, and looked round at the generals.

"Gentlemen, the dispositions for tomorrow—or rather for today, for it is past midnight—cannot now be altered," said he. "You have heard them, and we shall all do our duty. But before a battle, there is nothing more important..." he paused, "than to have a good sleep."

He moved as if to rise. The generals bowed and retired. It was past midnight. Prince Andrew went out.

The council of war, at which Prince Andrew had not been able to express his opinion as he had hoped to, left on him a vague and uneasy impression. Whether Dolgorúkov and Weyrother, or Kutúzov, Langeron, and the others who did not approve of the plan of attack, were right—he did not know. "But was it really not possible for Kutúzov to state his views plainly to the Emperor? Is it possible that on account of court and personal considerations tens of thousands of lives, and my life, *my* life," he thought, "must be risked?"

"Yes, it is very likely that I shall be killed tomorrow," he thought. And suddenly, at this thought of death, a whole series of most distant, most intimate, memories rose in his imagination: he remembered his last parting from his father and his wife; he remembered the days when he first loved her. He thought of her pregnancy and felt sorry for her and for himself, and in a nervously emotional and softened mood he went out of the hut in which he was billeted with Nesvítski and began to walk up and down before it.

The night was foggy and through the fog the moonlight gleamed mysteriously. "Yes, tomorrow, tomorrow!" he thought. "Tomorrow everything may be over for me! All these memories will be no more, none of them will have any meaning for me. Tomorrow perhaps, even certainly, I have a presentiment that for the first time I shall have to show all I can do." And his fancy pictured the battle, its loss, the concentration of fighting at one point, and the hesitation of all the commanders. And then that happy moment, that Toulon for which he had so long waited, presents itself to him at last. He firmly and clearly expresses his opinion to Kutúzov, to Weyrother, and to the Emperors. All are struck by the justness of his views, but no one undertakes to carry them out, so he takes a regiment, a division—stipulates that no one is to interfere with his arrangements—leads his division to the decisive point, and gains the victory alone. "But death and suffering?" suggested another voice. Prince Andrew, however, did not answer that voice and went on dreaming of his triumphs. The dispositions for the next battle are planned by him alone. Nominally he is only an adjutant on Kutúzov's staff, but he does everything alone. The next battle is won by him alone. Kutúzov is removed and he is appointed... "Well and then?" asked the other voice. "If before that you are not ten times wounded, killed, or betrayed, well... what then?..." "Well then," Prince Andrew answered himself, "I don't know what will happen and don't want to know, and can't, but if I want this—want glory, want to be known to men, want to be loved by them, it is not my fault that I want it and want nothing but that and live only for that. Yes, for that alone! I shall never tell anyone, but, oh God! what am I to do if I love nothing but fame and men's esteem? Death, wounds, the loss of family—I fear nothing. And precious and dear as many persons are to me—father, sister, wife—those dearest to me—yet dreadful and unnatural as it seems, I would give them all at once for a moment of glory, of triumph over men, of love from men I don't know and never shall know, for the love of these men here," he thought, as he listened to voices in Kutúzov's courtyard. The voices were those of the orderlies who were packing up; one voice, probably a coachman's, was teasing Kutúzov's old cook whom Prince Andrew knew, and who was called Tit. He was saying, "Tit, I say, Tit!"

"Well?" returned the old man.

"Go, Tit, thresh a bit!" said the wag.

"Oh, go to the devil!" called out a voice, drowned by the laughter of the orderlies and servants.

"All the same, I love and value nothing but triumph over them all, I value this mystic power and glory that is floating here above me in this mist!"

CHAPTER XIII

That same night, Rostóv was with a platoon on skirmishing duty in front of Bagratión's detachment. His hussars were placed along the line in couples and he himself rode along the line trying to master the sleepiness that kept coming over him. An enormous space, with our army's campfires dimly glowing in the fog, could be seen behind him; in front of him was misty darkness. Rostóv could see nothing, peer as he would into that foggy distance: now something gleamed gray, now there was something black, now little lights seemed to glimmer where the enemy ought to be, now he fancied it was only something in his own eyes. His eyes kept closing, and in his fancy appeared—now the Emperor, now Denísov, and now Moscow memories—and he again hurriedly opened his eyes and saw close before him the head and ears of the horse he was riding, and sometimes, when he came within six paces of them, the black figures of hussars, but in the distance was still the same misty darkness. "Why not?... It might easily happen," thought Rostóv, "that the Emperor will meet me and give me an order as he would to any other officer; he'll say: 'Go and find out what's there.' There are many stories of his getting to know an officer in just such a chance way and attaching him to himself! What if he gave me a place near him? Oh, how I would guard him, how I would tell him the truth, how I would unmask his deceivers!" And in order to realize vividly his love devotion to the sovereign, Rostóv pictured to himself an enemy or a deceitful German, whom he would not only kill with pleasure but whom he would slap in the face before the Emperor. Suddenly a distant shout aroused him. He started and opened his eyes.

"Where am I? Oh yes, in the skirmishing line... pass and watchword—*shaft, Olmütz*. What a nuisance that our squadron will be in reserve tomorrow," he thought. "I'll ask leave to go to the front, this may be my only chance of seeing the Emperor. It won't be long now before I am off duty. I'll take another turn and when I get back I'll go to the general and ask him." He readjusted himself in the saddle and touched up his horse to ride once more round his hussars. It seemed to him that it was getting lighter. To the left he saw a sloping descent lit up, and facing it a black knoll that seemed as steep as a wall. On this knoll there was a white patch that Rostóv could not at all make out: was it a glade in the wood lit up by the moon, or some unmelted snow, or some white houses? He even thought something moved on that white spot. "I expect it's snow... that spot... a spot—*unetache*," he thought. "There now... it's not a *tache*... Natásha... sister, black eyes... Na... tasha... (Won't she be surprised when I tell her how I've seen the Emperor?) Natásha... take my sabretache..."—"Keep to the right, your honor, there are bushes here," came the voice of an hussar, past whom Rostóv was riding in the act of falling asleep. Rostóv lifted his head that had sunk almost to his horse's mane and pulled up beside the hussar. He was succumbing to irresistible, youthful, childish drowsiness. "But what was I thinking? I mustn't forget. How shall I speak to the Emperor? No, that's not it—that's tomorrow. Oh yes! Natásha... sabretache... saber them... Whom? The hussars... Ah, the hussars with mustaches. Along the Tverskáya Street rode the hussar with mustaches... I thought about him too, just opposite Gúryev's house... Old Gúryev.... Oh, but Denísov's a fine fellow. But that's all nonsense. The chief thing is that the Emperor is here. How he looked at me and wished to say something, but dared not.... No, it was I who dared not. But that's nonsense, the chief thing is not to forget the important thing I was thinking of. Yes, Na-tásha, sabretache, oh, yes, yes! That's right!" And his head once more sank to his horse's neck. All at once it seemed to him that he was being fired at. "What? What? What?... Cut them down! What?..." said Rostóv, waking up. At the moment he opened his eyes he heard in front of him, where the enemy was, the long-drawn shouts of thousands of voices. His horse and the horse of the hussar near him pricked their ears at these shouts. Over there, where the shouting came from, a fire flared up and went out again, then another, and all along the French line on the hill fires flared up and the shouting grew louder and louder. Rostóv could hear the sound of French words but could not distinguish them. The din of many voices was too great; all he could hear was: "ahahah!" and "rrrr!"

"What's that? What do you make of it?" said Rostóv to the hussar beside him. "That must be the enemy's camp!"

The hussar did not reply.

"Why, don't you hear it?" Rostóv asked again, after waiting for a reply.

"Who can tell, your honor?" replied the hussar reluctantly.

"From the direction, it must be the enemy," repeated Rostóv.

"It may be *he* or it may be nothing," muttered the hussar. "It's dark... Steady!" he cried to his fidgeting horse.

Rostóv's horse was also getting restive: it pawed the frozen ground, pricking its ears at the noise and looking at the lights. The shouting grew still louder and merged into a general roar that only an army of several thousand men could produce. The lights spread farther and farther, probably along the line of the French camp. Rostóv no longer wanted to sleep. The gay triumphant shouting of the enemy army had a stimulating effect on him. *"Vivel'Empereur! l'Empereur!"* he now heard distinctly.

"They can't be far off, probably just beyond the stream," he said to the hussar beside him.

The hussar only sighed without replying and coughed angrily. The sound of horse's hoofs approaching at a trot along the line of hussars was heard, and out of the foggy darkness the figure of a sergeant of hussars suddenly appeared, looming huge as an elephant.

"Your honor, the generals!" said the sergeant, riding up to Rostóv.

Rostóv, still looking round toward the fires and the shouts, rode with the sergeant to meet some mounted men who were riding along the line. One was on a white horse. Prince Bagratión and Prince Dolgorúkov with their adjutants had come to witness the curious phenomenon of the lights and shouts in the enemy's camp. Rostóv rode up to Bagratión, reported to him, and then joined the adjutants listening to what the generals were saying.

"Believe me," said Prince Dolgorúkov, addressing Bagratión, "it is nothing but a trick! He has retreated and ordered the rearguard to kindle fires and make a noise to deceive us."

"Hardly," said Bagratión. "I saw them this evening on that knoll; if they had retreated they would have withdrawn from that too.... Officer!" said Bagratión to Rostóv, "are the enemy's skirmishers still there?"

"They were there this evening, but now I don't know, your excellency. Shall I go with some of my hussars to see?" replied Rostóv.

Bagratión stopped and, before replying, tried to see Rostóv's face in the mist.

"Well, go and see," he said, after a pause.

"Yes, sir."

Rostóv spurred his horse, called to Sergeant Fédchenko and two other hussars, told them to follow him, and trotted downhill in the direction from which the shouting came. He felt both frightened and pleased to be riding alone with three hussars into that mysterious and dangerous misty distance where no one had been before him. Bagratión called to him from the hill not to go beyond the stream, but Rostóv pretended not to hear him and did not stop but rode on and on, continually mistaking bushes for trees and gullies for men and continually discovering his mistakes. Having descended the hill at a trot, he no longer saw either our own or the enemy's fires, but heard the shouting of the French more loudly and distinctly. In the valley he saw before him something like a river, but when he reached it he found it was a road. Having come out onto the road he reined in his horse, hesitating whether to ride along it or cross it and ride over the black field up the hillside. To keep to the road which gleamed white in the mist would have been safer because it would be easier to see people coming along it. "Follow me!" said he, crossed the road, and began riding up the hill at a gallop toward the point where the French pickets had been standing that evening.

"Your honor, there he is!" cried one of the hussars behind him. And before Rostóv had time to make out what the black thing was that had suddenly appeared in the fog, there was a flash, followed by a report, and a bullet whizzing high up in the mist with a plaintive sound passed out of hearing. Another musket missed fire but flashed in the pan. Rostóv turned his horse and galloped back. Four more reports followed at intervals, and the bullets passed somewhere in the fog singing in different tones. Rostóv reined in his horse, whose spirits had risen, like his own, at the firing, and went back at a footpace. "Well, some more! Some more!" a merry voice was saying in his soul. But no more shots came.

Only when approaching Bagratión did Rostóv let his horse gallop again, and with his hand at the salute rode up to the general.

Dolgorúkov was still insisting that the French had retreated and had only lit fires to deceive us.

"What does that prove?" he was saying as Rostóv rode up. "They might retreat and leave the pickets."

"It's plain that they have not all gone yet, Prince," said Bagratión. "Wait till tomorrow morning, we'll find out everything tomorrow."

"The picket is still on the hill, your excellency, just where it was in the evening," reported Rostóv, stooping forward with his hand at the salute and unable to repress the smile of delight induced by his ride and especially by the sound of the bullets.

"Very good, very good," said Bagratión. "Thank you, officer."

"Your excellency," said Rostóv, "may I ask a favor?"

"What is it?"

"Tomorrow our squadron is to be in reserve. May I ask to be attached to the first squadron?"

"What's your name?"

"Count Rostóv."

"Oh, very well, you may stay in attendance on me."

"Count IlyáRostóv's son?" asked Dolgorúkov.

But Rostóv did not reply.

"Then I may reckon on it, your excellency?"

"I will give the order."

"Tomorrow very likely I may be sent with some message to the Emperor," thought Rostóv.

"Thank God!"

The fires and shouting in the enemy's army were occasioned by the fact that while Napoleon's proclamation was being read to the troops the Emperor himself rode round his bivouacs. The soldiers, on seeing him, lit wisps of straw and ran after him, shouting, *"Vivel'Empereur!"* Napoleon's proclamation was as follows:

Soldiers! The Russian army is advancing against you to avenge the Austrian army of Ulm. They are the same battalions you broke at Hollabrünn and have pursued ever since to this place. The position we occupy is a strong one, and while they are marching to go round me on the right they will expose a flank to me. Soldiers! I will myself direct your battalions. I will keep out of fire if you with your habitual valor carry disorder and confusion into the enemy's ranks, but should victory be in doubt, even for a moment, you will see your Emperor exposing himself to the first blows of the enemy, for there must be no doubt of victory, especially on this day when what is at stake is the honor of the French infantry, so necessary to the honor of our nation.

Do not break your ranks on the plea of removing the wounded! Let every man be fully imbued with the thought that we must defeat these hirelings of England, inspired by such hatred of our nation! This victory will conclude our campaign and we can return to winter quarters, where fresh French troops who are being raised in France will join us, and the peace I shall conclude will be worthy of my people, of you, and of myself.

NAPOLEON

CHAPTER XIV

At five in the morning it was still quite dark. The troops of the center, the reserves, and Bagratión's right flank had not yet moved, but on the left flank the columns of infantry, cavalry, and artillery, which were to be the first to descend the heights to attack the French right flank and drive it into the Bohemian mountains according to plan, were already up and astir. The smoke of the campfires, into which they were throwing everything superfluous, made the eyes smart. It was cold and dark. The officers were hurriedly drinking tea and breakfasting, the soldiers, munching biscuit and beating a tattoo with their feet to warm themselves, gathering round the fires throwing into the flames the remains of sheds, chairs, tables, wheels, tubs, and everything that they did not want or could not carry away with them. Austrian column guides were moving in and out among the Russian troops and served as heralds of the advance. As soon as an Austrian officer showed himself near a commanding officer's quarters, the regiment began to move: the soldiers ran from the fires, thrust their pipes into their boots, their bags into the carts, got their muskets ready, and formed rank. The officers buttoned up their coats, buckled on their swords and pouches, and moved along the ranks shouting. The train drivers and orderlies harnessed and packed the wagons and tied on the loads. The adjutants and battalion and regimental commanders mounted, crossed themselves, gave final instructions, orders, and commissions to the baggage men who remained behind, and the monotonous tramp of thousands of feet resounded. The column moved forward without knowing where and unable, from the masses around them, the smoke and the increasing fog, to see either the place they were leaving or that to which they were going.

A soldier on the march is hemmed in and borne along by his regiment as much as a sailor is by his ship. However far he has walked, whatever strange, unknown, and dangerous places he reaches, just as a sailor is always surrounded by the same decks, masts, and rigging of his ship, so the soldier always has around him the same comrades, the same ranks, the same sergeant major Iván Mítrich, the same company dog Jack, and the same commanders. The sailor rarely cares to know the latitude in which his ship is sailing, but on the day of battle—heaven knows how and whence—a stern note of which all are conscious sounds in the moral atmosphere of an army, announcing the approach of something decisive and solemn, and awakening in the men an unusual curiosity. On the day of battle the soldiers excitedly try to get beyond the interests of their regiment, they listen intently, look about, and eagerly ask concerning what is going on around them.

The fog had grown so dense that though it was growing light they could not see ten paces ahead. Bushes looked like gigantic trees and level ground like cliffs and slopes. Anywhere, on any side, one might encounter an enemy invisible ten paces off. But the columns advanced for a long time, always in the same fog, descending and ascending hills, avoiding gardens and enclosures, going over new and unknown ground, and nowhere encountering the enemy. On the contrary, the soldiers became aware that in front, behind, and on all sides, other Russian columns were moving in the same direction. Every soldier felt glad to know that to the unknown place where he was going, many more of our men were going too.

"There now, the Kúrskies have also gone past," was being said in the ranks.

"It's wonderful what a lot of our troops have gathered, lads! Last night I looked at the campfires and there was no end of them. A regular Moscow!"

Though none of the column commanders rode up to the ranks or talked to the men (the commanders, as we saw at the council of war, were out of humor and dissatisfied with the affair, and so did not exert themselves to cheer the men but merely carried out the orders), yet the troops marched gaily, as they always do when going into action, especially to an attack. But when they had marched for about an hour in the dense fog, the greater part of the men had to halt and an unpleasant consciousness of some dislocation and blunder spread through the ranks. How such a consciousness is communicated is very difficult to define, but it certainly is communicated very surely, and flows rapidly, imperceptibly, and irrepressibly, as water does in a creek. Had the Russian army been alone without any allies, it might perhaps have been a long time before this consciousness of mismanagement became a general conviction, but as it was, the disorder was readily and naturally attributed to the stupid Germans, and everyone was convinced that a dangerous muddle had been occasioned by the sausage eaters.

"Why have we stopped? Is the way blocked? Or have we already come up against the French?"

"No, one can't hear them. They'd be firing if we had."

"They were in a hurry enough to start us, and now here we stand in the middle of a field without rhyme or reason. It's all those damned Germans' muddling! What stupid devils!"

"Yes, I'd send them on in front, but no fear, they're crowding up behind. And now here we stand hungry."

"I say, shall we soon be clear? They say the cavalry are blocking the way," said an officer.

"Ah, those damned Germans! They don't know their own country!" said another.

"What division are you?" shouted an adjutant, riding up.

"The Eighteenth."

"Then why are you here? You should have gone on long ago, now you won't get there till evening."

"What stupid orders! They don't themselves know what they are doing!" said the officer and rode off.

Then a general rode past shouting something angrily, not in Russian.

"Tafa-lafa! But what he's jabbering no one can make out," said a soldier, mimicking the general who had ridden away. "I'd shoot them, the scoundrels!"

"We were ordered to be at the place before nine, but we haven't got halfway. Fine orders!" was being repeated on different sides.

And the feeling of energy with which the troops had started began to turn into vexation and anger at the stupid arrangements and at the Germans.

The cause of the confusion was that while the Austrian cavalry was moving toward our left flank, the higher command found that our center was too far separated from our right flank and the cavalry were all ordered to turn back to the right. Several thousand cavalry crossed in front of the infantry, who had to wait.

At the front an altercation occurred between an Austrian guide and a Russian general. The general shouted a demand that the cavalry should be halted, the Austrian argued that not he, but the higher command, was to blame. The troops meanwhile stood growing listless and dispirited. After an hour's delay they at last moved on, descending the hill. The fog that was dispersing on the hill lay still more densely below, where they were descending. In front in the fog a shot was heard and then another, at first irregularly at varying intervals—trata...tat—and then more and more regularly and rapidly, and the action at the Goldbach Stream began.

Not expecting to come on the enemy down by the stream, and having stumbled on him in the fog, hearing no encouraging word from their commanders, and with a consciousness of being too late spreading through the ranks, and above all being unable to see anything in front or around them in the thick fog, the Russians exchanged shots with the enemy lazily and advanced and again halted, receiving no timely orders from the officers or adjutants who wandered about in the fog in those unknown surroundings unable to find their own regiments. In this way the action began for the first, second, and third columns, which had gone down into the valley. The fourth column, with which Kutúzov was, stood on the Pratzen Heights.

Below, where the fight was beginning, there was still thick fog; on the higher ground it was clearing, but nothing could be seen of what was going on in front. Whether all the enemy forces were, as we supposed, six miles away, or whether they were near by in that sea of mist, no one knew till after eight o'clock.

It was nine o'clock in the morning. The fog lay unbroken like a sea down below, but higher up at the village of Schlappanitz where Napoleon stood with his marshals around him, it was quite light. Above him was a clear blue sky, and the sun's vast orb quivered like a huge hollow, crimson float on the surface of that milky sea of mist. The whole French army, and even Napoleon himself with his staff, were not on the far side of the streams and hollows of Sokolnitz and Schlappanitz beyond which we intended to take up our position and begin the action, but were on this side, so close to our own forces that Napoleon with the naked eye could distinguish a mounted man from one on foot. Napoleon, in the blue cloak which he had worn on his Italian campaign, sat on his small gray Arab horse a little in front of his marshals. He gazed silently at the hills which seemed to rise out of the sea of mist and on which the Russian troops were moving in the distance, and he listened to the sounds of firing in the valley. Not a single muscle of his face—which in those days was still thin—moved. His gleaming eyes were fixed intently on one spot. His predictions were being justified. Part of the Russian force had already descended into the valley toward the ponds and lakes and part were leaving these Pratzen Heights which he intended to attack and regarded as the key to the position. He saw over the mist that in a hollow between two hills near the village of Pratzen, the Russian columns, their bayonets glittering, were moving continuously in one direction toward the valley and disappearing one after another into the mist. From information he had received the evening before, from the sound of wheels and footsteps heard by the outposts during the night, by the disorderly movement of the Russian columns, and from all indications, he saw clearly that the allies believed him to be far away in front of them, and that the columns moving near Pratzen constituted the center of the Russian army, and that that center was already sufficiently weakened to be successfully attacked. But still he did not begin the engagement.

Today was a great day for him—the anniversary of his coronation. Before dawn he had slept for a few hours, and refreshed, vigorous, and in good spirits, he mounted his horse and rode out into the field in that happy mood in which everything seems possible and everything succeeds. He sat motionless, looking at the heights visible above the mist, and his cold face wore that special look of confident, self-complacent happiness that one sees on the face of a boy happily in love. The marshals stood behind him not venturing to distract his attention. He looked now at the Pratzen Heights, now at the sun floating up out of the mist.

When the sun had entirely emerged from the fog, and fields and mist were aglow with dazzling light—as if he had only awaited this to begin the action—he drew the glove from his shapely white hand, made a sign with it to the marshals, and ordered the action to begin. The marshals, accompanied by adjutants, galloped off in different directions, and a few minutes later the chief forces of the French army moved rapidly toward those Pratzen Heights which were being more and more denuded by Russian troops moving down the valley to their left.

CHAPTER XV

At eight o'clock Kutúzov rode to Pratzen at the head of the fourth column, Milorádovich's, the one that was to take the place of Przebyszéwski's and Langeron's columns which had already gone down into the valley. He greeted the men of the foremost regiment and gave them the order to march, thereby indicating that he intended to lead that column himself. When he had reached the village of Pratzen he halted. Prince Andrew was behind, among the immense number forming the commander in chief's suite. He was in a state of suppressed excitement and irritation, though controlledly calm as a man is at the approach of a long-awaited moment. He was firmly convinced that this was the day of his Toulon, or his bridge of Arcola. How it would come about he did not know, but he felt sure it would do so. The locality and the position of our troops were known to him as far as they could be known to anyone in our army. His own strategic plan, which obviously could not now be carried out, was forgotten. Now, entering into Weyrother's plan, Prince Andrew considered possible contingencies and formed new projects such as might call for his rapidity of perception and decision.

To the left down below in the mist, the musketry fire of unseen forces could be heard. It was there Prince Andrew thought the fight would concentrate. "There we shall encounter difficulties, and there," thought he, "I shall be sent with a brigade or division, and there, standard in hand, I shall go forward and break whatever is in front of me."

He could not look calmly at the standards of the passing battalions. Seeing them he kept thinking, "That may be the very standard with which I shall lead the army."

In the morning all that was left of the night mist on the heights was a hoar frost now turning to dew, but in the valleys it still lay like a milk-white sea. Nothing was visible in the valley to the left into which our troops had descended and from whence came the sounds of firing. Above the heights was the dark clear sky, and to the right the vast orb of the sun. In front, far off on the farther shore of that sea of mist, some wooded hills were discernible, and it was there the enemy probably was, for something could be descried. On the right the Guards were entering the misty region with a sound of hoofs and wheels and now and then a gleam of bayonets; to the left beyond the village similar masses of cavalry came up and disappeared in the sea of mist. In front and behind moved infantry. The commander in chief was standing at the end of the village letting the troops pass by him. That morning Kutúzov seemed worn and irritable. The infantry passing before him came to a halt without any command being given, apparently obstructed by something in front.

"Do order them to form into battalion columns and go round the village!" he said angrily to a general who had ridden up. "Don't you understand, your excellency, my dear sir, that you must not defile through narrow village streets when we are marching against the enemy?"

"I intended to re-form them beyond the village, your excellency," answered the general.

Kutúzov laughed bitterly.

"You'll make a fine thing of it, deploying in sight of the enemy! Very fine!"

"The enemy is still far away, your excellency. According to the dispositions..."

"The dispositions!" exclaimed Kutúzov bitterly. "Who told you that?... Kindly do as you are ordered."

"Yes, sir."

"My dear fellow," Nesvítski whispered to Prince Andrew, "the old man is as surly as a dog."

An Austrian officer in a white uniform with green plumes in his hat galloped up to Kutúzov and asked in the Emperor's name had the fourth column advanced into action.

Kutúzov turned round without answering and his eye happened to fall upon Prince Andrew, who was beside him. Seeing him, Kutúzov's malevolent and caustic expression softened, as if admitting that what was being done was not his adjutant's fault, and still not answering the Austrian adjutant, he addressed Bolkónski.

"Go, my dear fellow, and see whether the third division has passed the village. Tell it to stop and await my orders."

Hardly had Prince Andrew started than he stopped him.

"And ask whether sharpshooters have been posted," he added. "What are they doing? What are they doing?" he murmured to himself, still not replying to the Austrian.

Prince Andrew galloped off to execute the order.

Overtaking the battalions that continued to advance, he stopped the third division and convinced himself that there really were no sharpshooters in front of our columns. The colonel at the head of the regiment was much surprised at the commander in chief's order to throw out skirmishers. He had felt perfectly sure that there were other troops in front of him and that the enemy must be at least six miles away. There was really nothing to be seen in front except a barren descent hidden by dense mist. Having given orders in the commander in chief's name to rectify this omission, Prince Andrew galloped back. Kutúzov still in the same place, his stout body resting heavily in the saddle with the lassitude of age, sat yawning wearily with closed eyes. The troops were no longer moving, but stood with the butts of their muskets on the ground.

"All right, all right!" he said to Prince Andrew, and turned to a general who, watch in hand, was saying it was time they started as all the left-flank columns had already descended.

"Plenty of time, your excellency," muttered Kutúzov in the midst of a yawn. "Plenty of time," he repeated.

Just then at a distance behind Kutúzov was heard the sound of regiments saluting, and this sound rapidly came nearer along the whole extended line of the advancing Russian columns. Evidently the person they were greeting was riding quickly. When the soldiers of the regiment in front of which Kutúzov was standing began to shout, he rode a little to one side and looked round with a frown. Along the road from Pratzen galloped what looked like a squadron of horsemen in various uniforms. Two of them rode side by side in front, at full gallop. One in a black uniform with white plumes in his hat rode a bobtailed chestnut horse, the other who was in a white uniform rode a black one. These were the two Emperors followed by their suites. Kutúzov, affecting the manners of an old soldier at the front, gave the command "Attention!" and rode up to the Emperors with a salute. His whole appearance and manner were suddenly transformed. He put on the air of a subordinate who obeys without reasoning. With an affectation of respect which evidently struck Alexander unpleasantly, he rode up and saluted.

This unpleasant impression merely flitted over the young and happy face of the Emperor like a cloud of haze across a clear sky and vanished. After his illness he looked rather thinner that day than on the field of Olmütz where Bolkónski had seen him for the first time abroad, but there was still the same bewitching combination of majesty and mildness in his fine gray eyes, and on his delicate lips the same capacity for varying expression and the same prevalent appearance of goodhearted innocent youth.

At the Olmütz review he had seemed more majestic; here he seemed brighter and more energetic. He was slightly flushed after galloping two miles, and reining in his horse he sighed restfully and looked round at the faces of his suite, young and animated as his own. Czartorýski, Novosíltsev, Prince Volkónsky, Strógonov, and the others, all richly dressed gay young men on splendid, well-groomed, fresh, only slightly heated horses, exchanging remarks and smiling, had stopped behind the Emperor. The Emperor Francis, a rosy, long faced young man, sat very erect on his handsome black horse, looking about him in a leisurely and preoccupied manner. He beckoned to one of his white adjutants and asked some question—"Most likely he is asking at what o'clock they started," thought Prince Andrew, watching his old acquaintance with a smile he could not repress as he recalled his reception at Brünn. In the Emperors' suite were the picked young orderly officers of the Guard and line regiments, Russian and Austrian. Among them were grooms leading the Tsar's beautiful relay horses covered with embroidered cloths.

As when a window is opened a whiff of fresh air from the fields enters a stuffy room, so a whiff of youthfulness, energy, and confidence of success reached Kutúzov's cheerless staff with the galloping advent of all these brilliant young men.

"Why aren't you beginning, Michael Ilariónovich?" said the Emperor Alexander hurriedly to Kutúzov, glancing courteously at the same time at the Emperor Francis.

"I am waiting, Your Majesty," answered Kutúzov, bending forward respectfully.

The Emperor, frowning slightly, bent his ear forward as if he had not quite heard.

"Waiting, Your Majesty," repeated Kutúzov. (Prince Andrew noted that Kutúzov's upper lip twitched unnaturally as he said the word "waiting.") "Not all the columns have formed up yet, Your Majesty."

The Tsar heard but obviously did not like the reply; he shrugged his rather round shoulders and glanced at Novosíltsev who was near him, as if complaining of Kutúzov.

"You know, Michael Ilariónovich, we are not on the Empress' Field where a parade does not begin till all the troops are assembled," said the Tsar with another glance at the Emperor Francis, as if inviting him if not to join in at least to listen to what he was saying. But the Emperor Francis continued to look about him and did not listen.

"That is just why I do not begin, sire," said Kutúzov in a resounding voice, apparently to preclude the possibility of not being heard, and again something in his face twitched—"That is just why I do not begin, sire, because we are not on parade and not on the Empress' Field," said he clearly and distinctly.

In the Emperor's suite all exchanged rapid looks that expressed dissatisfaction and reproach. "Old though he may be, he should not, he certainly should not, speak like that," their glances seemed to say.

The Tsar looked intently and observantly into Kutúzov's eye waiting to hear whether he would say anything more. But Kutúzov, with respectfully bowed head, seemed also to be waiting. The silence lasted for about a minute.

"However, if you command it, Your Majesty," said Kutúzov, lifting his head and again assuming his former tone of a dull, unreasoning, but submissive general.

He touched his horse and having called Milorádovich, the commander of the column, gave him the order to advance.

The troops again began to move, and two battalions of the Nóvgorod and one of the Ápsheron regiment went forward past the Emperor.

As this Ápsheron battalion marched by, the red-faced Milorádovich, without his greatcoat, with his Orders on his breast and an enormous tuft of plumes in his cocked hat worn on one side with its corners front and back, galloped strenuously forward, and with a dashing salute reined in his horse before the Emperor.

"God be with you, general!" said the Emperor.

"*Ma foi, sire, nous feronsce qui sera dans notrepossibilité, sire,*" * he answered gaily, raising nevertheless ironic smiles among the gentlemen of the Tsar's suite by his poor French.

* "Indeed, Sire, we shall do everything it is possible to do, Sire."

Milorádovich wheeled his horse sharply and stationed himself a little behind the Emperor. The Ápsheron men, excited by the Tsar's presence, passed in step before the Emperors and their suites at a bold, brisk pace.

"Lads!" shouted Milorádovich in a loud, self-confident, and cheery voice, obviously so elated by the sound of firing, by the prospect of battle, and by the sight of the gallant Ápsherons, his comrades in Suvórov's time, now passing so gallantly before the Emperors, that he forgot the sovereigns' presence. "Lads, it's not the first village you've had to take," cried he.

"Glad to do our best!" shouted the soldiers.

The Emperor's horse started at the sudden cry. This horse that had carried the sovereign at reviews in Russia bore him also here on the field of Austerlitz, enduring the heedless blows of his left foot and pricking its ears at the sound of shots just as it had done on the Empress' Field, not understanding the significance of the firing, nor of the nearness of the Emperor Francis' black cob, nor of all that was being said, thought, and felt that day by its rider.

The Emperor turned with a smile to one of his followers and made a remark to him, pointing to the gallant Ápsherons.

CHAPTER XVI

Kutúzov accompanied by his adjutants rode at a walking pace behind the carabineers.

When he had gone less than half a mile in the rear of the column he stopped at a solitary, deserted house that had probably once been an inn, where two roads parted. Both of them led downhill and troops were marching along both.

The fog had begun to clear and enemy troops were already dimly visible about a mile and a half off on the opposite heights. Down below, on the left, the firing became more distinct. Kutúzov had stopped and was speaking to an Austrian general. Prince Andrew, who was a little behind looking at them, turned to an adjutant to ask him for a field glass.

"Look, look!" said this adjutant, looking not at the troops in the distance, but down the hill before him. "It's the French!"

The two generals and the adjutant took hold of the field glass, trying to snatch it from one another. The expression on all their faces suddenly changed to one of horror. The French were supposed to be a mile and a half away, but had suddenly and unexpectedly appeared just in front of us.

"It's the enemy?... No!... Yes, see it is!... for certain.... But how is that?" said different voices.

With the naked eye Prince Andrew saw below them to the right, not more than five hundred paces from where Kutúzov was standing, a dense French column coming up to meet the Ápsherons.

"Here it is! The decisive moment has arrived. My turn has come," thought Prince Andrew, and striking his horse he rode up to Kutúzov.

"The Ápsherons must be stopped, your excellency," cried he. But at that very instant a cloud of smoke spread all round, firing was heard quite close at hand, and a voice of naïve terror barely two steps from Prince Andrew shouted, "Brothers! All's lost!" And at this as if at a command, everyone began to run.

Confused and ever-increasing crowds were running back to where five minutes before the troops had passed the Emperors. Not only would it have been difficult to stop that crowd, it was even impossible not to be carried back with it oneself. Bolkónski only tried not to lose touch with it, and looked around bewildered and unable to grasp what was happening in front of him. Nesvítski with an angry face, red and unlike himself, was shouting to Kutúzovthat if he did not ride away at once he would certainly be taken prisoner. Kutúzov remained in the same place and without answering drew out a handkerchief. Blood was flowing from his cheek. Prince Andrew forced his way to him.

"You are wounded?" he asked, hardly able to master the trembling of his lower jaw.

"The wound is not here, it is there!" said Kutúzov, pressing the handkerchief to his wounded cheek and pointing to the fleeing soldiers. "Stop them!" he shouted, and at the same moment, probably realizing that it was impossible to stop them, spurred his horse and rode to the right.

A fresh wave of the flying mob caught him and bore him back with it.

The troops were running in such a dense mass that once surrounded by them it was difficult to get out again. One was shouting, "Get on! Why are you hindering us?" Another in the same place turned round and fired in the air; a third was striking the horse Kutúzov himself rode. Having by a great effort got away to the left from that flood of men, Kutúzov, with his suite diminished by more than half, rode toward a sound of artillery fire near by. Having forced his way out of the crowd of fugitives, Prince Andrew, trying to keep near Kutúzov, saw on the slope of the hill amid the smoke a Russian battery that was still firing and Frenchmen running toward it. Higher up stood some Russian infantry, neither moving forward to protect the battery nor backward with the fleeing crowd. A mounted general separated himself from the infantry and approached Kutúzov. Of Kutúzov's suite only four remained. They were all pale and exchanged looks in silence.

"Stop those wretches!" gasped Kutúzov to the regimental commander, pointing to the flying soldiers; but at that instant, as if to punish him for those words, bullets flew hissing across the regiment and across Kutúzov's suite like a flock of little birds.

The French had attacked the battery and, seeing Kutúzov, were firing at him. After this volley the regimental commander clutched at his leg; several soldiers fell, and a second lieutenant who was holding the flag let it fall from his hands. It swayed and fell, but caught on the muskets of the nearest soldiers. The soldiers started firing without orders.

"Oh! Oh! Oh!" groaned Kutúzov despairingly and looked around.... "Bolkónski!" he whispered, his voice trembling from a consciousness of the feebleness of age, "Bolkónski!" he whispered, pointing to the disordered battalion and at the enemy, "what's that?"

But before he had finished speaking, Prince Andrew, feeling tears of shame and anger choking him, had already leapt from his horse and run to the standard.

"Forward, lads!" he shouted in a voice piercing as a child's.

"Here it is!" thought he, seizing the staff of the standard and hearing with pleasure the whistle of bullets evidently aimed at him. Several soldiers fell.

"Hurrah!" shouted Prince Andrew, and, scarcely able to hold up the heavy standard, he ran forward with full confidence that the whole battalion would follow him.

And really he only ran a few steps alone. One soldier moved and then another and soon the whole battalion ran forward shouting "Hurrah!" and overtook him. A sergeant of the battalion ran up and took the flag that was swaying from its weight in Prince Andrew's hands, but he was immediately killed. Prince Andrew again seized the standard and, dragging it by the staff, ran on with the battalion. In front he saw our artillerymen, some of whom were fighting, while others, having abandoned their guns, were running toward him. He also saw French infantry soldiers who were seizing the artillery horses and turning the guns round. Prince Andrew and the battalion were already within twenty paces of the cannon. He heard the whistle of bullets above him unceasingly and to right and left of him soldiers continually groaned and dropped. But he did not look at them: he looked only at what was going on in front of him—at the battery. He now saw clearly the figure of a red-haired gunner with his shako knocked awry, pulling one end of a mop while a French soldier tugged at the other. He could distinctly see the distraught yet angry expression on the faces of these two men, who evidently did not realize what they were doing.

"What are they about?" thought Prince Andrew as he gazed at them. "Why doesn't the red-haired gunner run away as he is unarmed? Why doesn't the Frenchman stab him? He will not get away before the Frenchman remembers his bayonet and stabs him...."

And really another French soldier, trailing his musket, ran up to the struggling men, and the fate of the red-haired gunner, who had triumphantly secured the mop and still did not realize what awaited him, was about to be decided. But Prince Andrew did not see how it ended. It seemed to him as though one of the soldiers near him hit him on the head with the full swing of a bludgeon. It hurt a little, but the worst of it was that the pain distracted him and prevented his seeing what he had been looking at.

"What's this? Am I falling? My legs are giving way," thought he, and fell on his back. He opened his eyes, hoping to see how the struggle of the Frenchmen with the gunners ended, whether the red-haired gunner had been killed or not and whether the cannon had been captured or saved. But he saw nothing. Above him there was now nothing but the sky—the lofty sky, not clear yet still immeasurably lofty, with gray clouds gliding slowly across it. "How quiet, peaceful, and solemn; not at all as I ran," thought Prince Andrew—"not as we ran, shouting and fighting, not at all as the gunner and the Frenchman with frightened and angry faces struggled for the mop: how differently do those clouds glide across that lofty infinite sky! How was it I did not see that lofty sky before? And how happy I am to have found it at last! Yes! All is vanity, all falsehood, except that infinite sky. There is nothing, nothing, but that. But even it does not exist, there is nothing but quiet and peace. Thank God!..."

CHAPTER XVII

On our right flank commanded by Bagratión, at nine o'clock the battle had not yet begun. Not wishing to agree to Dolgorúkov's demand to commence the action, and wishing to avert responsibility from himself, Prince Bagratión proposed to Dolgorúkov to send to inquire of the commander in chief. Bagratión knew that as the distance between the two flanks was more than six miles, even if the messenger were not killed (which he very likely would be), and found the commander in chief (which would be very difficult), he would not be able to get back before evening.

Bagratión cast his large, expressionless, sleepy eyes round his suite, and the boyish face of Rostóv, breathless with excitement and hope, was the first to catch his eye. He sent him.

"And if I should meet His Majesty before I meet the commander in chief, your excellency?" said Rostóv, with his hand to his cap.

"You can give the message to His Majesty," said Dolgorúkov, hurriedly interrupting Bagratión.

On being relieved from picket duty Rostóv had managed to get a few hours' sleep before morning and felt cheerful, bold, and resolute, with elasticity of movement, faith in his good fortune, and generally in that state of mind which makes everything seem possible, pleasant, and easy.

All his wishes were being fulfilled that morning: there was to be a general engagement in which he was taking part, more than that, he was orderly to the bravest general, and still more, he was going with a message to Kutúzov, perhaps even to the sovereign himself. The morning was bright, he had a good horse under him, and his heart was full of joy and happiness. On receiving the order he gave his horse the rein and galloped along the line. At first he rode along the line of Bagratión's troops, which had not yet advanced into action but were standing motionless; then he came to the region occupied by Uvárov's cavalry and here he noticed a stir and signs of preparation for battle; having passed Uvárov's cavalry he clearly heard the sound of cannon and musketry ahead of him. The firing grew louder and louder.

In the fresh morning air were now heard, not two or three musket shots at irregular intervals as before, followed by one or two cannon shots, but a roll of volleys of musketry from the slopes of the hill before Pratzen, interrupted by such frequent reports of cannon that sometimes several of them were not separated from one another but merged into a general roar.

He could see puffs of musketry smoke that seemed to chase one another down the hillsides, and clouds of cannon smoke rolling, spreading, and mingling with one another. He could also, by the gleam of bayonets visible through the smoke, make out moving masses of infantry and narrow lines of artillery with green caissons.

Rostóv stopped his horse for a moment on a hillock to see what was going on, but strain his attention as he would he could not understand or make out anything of what was happening: there in the smoke men of some sort were moving about, in front and behind moved lines of troops; but why, whither, and who they were, it was impossible to make out. These sights and sounds had no depressing or intimidating effect on him; on the contrary, they stimulated his energy and determination.

"Go on! Go on! Give it them!" he mentally exclaimed at these sounds, and again proceeded to gallop along the line, penetrating farther and farther into the region where the army was already in action.

"How it will be there I don't know, but all will be well!" thought Rostóv.

After passing some Austrian troops he noticed that the next part of the line (the Guards) was already in action.

"So much the better! I shall see it close," he thought.

He was riding almost along the front line. A handful of men came galloping toward him. They were our Uhlans who with disordered ranks were returning from the attack. Rostóv got out of their way, involuntarily noticed that one of them was bleeding, and galloped on.

"That is no business of mine," he thought. He had not ridden many hundred yards after that before he saw to his left, across the whole width of the field, an enormous mass of cavalry in brilliant white uniforms, mounted on black horses, trotting straight toward him and across his path. Rostóv put his horse to full gallop to get out of the way of these men, and he would have got clear had they continued at the same speed, but they kept increasing their pace, so that some of the horses were already galloping. Rostóv heard the thud of their hoofs and the jingle of their weapons and saw their horses, their figures, and even their faces, more and more distinctly. They were our Horse Guards, advancing to attack the French cavalry that was coming to meet them.

The Horse Guards were galloping, but still holding in their horses. Rostóv could already see their faces and heard the command: "Charge!" shouted by an officer who was urging his thoroughbred to full speed. Rostóv, fearing to be crushed or swept into the attack on the French, galloped along the front as hard as his horse could go, but still was not in time to avoid them.

The last of the Horse Guards, a huge pockmarked fellow, frowned angrily on seeing Rostóv before him, with whom he would inevitably collide. This Guardsman would certainly have bowled Rostóv and his Bedouin over (Rostóv felt himself quite tiny and weak compared to these gigantic men and horses) had it not occurred to Rostóv to flourish his whip before the eyes of the Guardsman's horse. The heavy black horse, sixteen hands high, shied, throwing back its ears; but the pockmarked Guardsman drove his huge spurs in violently, and the horse, flourishing its tail and extending its neck, galloped on yet faster. Hardly had the Horse Guards passed Rostóv before he heard them shout, "Hurrah!" and looking back saw that their foremost ranks were mixed up with some foreign cavalry with red epaulets, probably French. He could see nothing more, for immediately afterwards cannon began firing from somewhere and smoke enveloped everything.

At that moment, as the Horse Guards, having passed him, disappeared in the smoke, Rostóv hesitated whether to gallop after them or to go where he was sent. This was the brilliant charge of the Horse Guards that amazed the French themselves. Rostóv was horrified to hear later that of all that mass of huge and handsome men, of all those brilliant, rich youths, officers and cadets, who had galloped past him on their thousand-ruble horses, only eighteen were left after the charge.

"Why should I envy them? My chance is not lost, and maybe I shall see the Emperor immediately!" thought Rostóv and galloped on.

When he came level with the Foot Guards he noticed that about them and around them cannon balls were flying, of which he was aware not so much because he heard their sound as because he saw uneasiness on the soldiers' faces and unnatural warlike solemnity on those of the officers.

Passing behind one of the lines of a regiment of Foot Guards he heard a voice calling him by name.

"Rostóv!"

"What?" he answered, not recognizing Borís.

"I say, we've been in the front line! Our regiment attacked!" said Borís with the happy smile seen on the faces of young men who have been under fire for the first time.

Rostóv stopped.

"Have you?" he said. "Well, how did it go?"

"We drove them back!" said Borís with animation, growing talkative. "Can you imagine it?" and he began describing how the Guards, having taken up their position and seeing troops before them, thought they were Austrians, and all at once discovered from the cannon balls discharged by those troops that they were themselves in the front line and had unexpectedly to go into action. Rostóv without hearing Borís to the end spurred his horse.

"Where are you off to?" asked Borís.

"With a message to His Majesty."

"There he is!" said Borís, thinking Rostóv had said "His Highness," and pointing to the Grand Duke who with his high shoulders and frowning brows stood a hundred paces away from them in his helmet and Horse Guards' jacket, shouting something to a pale, white uniformed Austrian officer.

"But that's the Grand Duke, and I want the commander in chief or the Emperor," said Rostóv, and was about to spur his horse.

"Count! Count!" shouted Berg who ran up from the other side as eager as Borís. "Count! I am wounded in my right hand" (and he showed his bleeding hand with a handkerchief tied round it) "and I remained at the front. I held my sword in my left hand, Count. All our family—the von Bergs—have been knights!"

He said something more, but Rostóv did not wait to hear it and rode away.

Having passed the Guards and traversed an empty space, Rostóv, to avoid again getting in front of the first line as he had done when the Horse Guards charged, followed the line of reserves, going far round the place where the hottest musket fire and cannonade were heard. Suddenly he heard musket fire quite close in front of him and behind our troops, where he could never have expected the enemy to be.

"What can it be?" he thought. "The enemy in the rear of our army? Impossible!" And suddenly he was seized by a panic of fear for himself and for the issue of the whole battle. "But be that what it may," he reflected, "there is no riding round it now. I must look for the commander in chief here, and if all is lost it is for me to perish with the rest."

The foreboding of evil that had suddenly come over Rostóv was more and more confirmed the farther he rode into the region behind the village of Pratzen, which was full of troops of all kinds.

"What does it mean? What is it? Whom are they firing at? Who is firing?" Rostóv kept asking as he came up to Russian and Austrian soldiers running in confused crowds across his path.

"The devil knows! They've killed everybody! It's all up now!" he was told in Russian, German, and Czech by the crowd of fugitives who understood what was happening as little as he did.

"Kill the Germans!" shouted one.

"May the devil take them—the traitors!"

"*ZumHenkerdieseRussen!*"* muttered a German.

* "Hang these Russians!"

Several wounded men passed along the road, and words of abuse, screams, and groans mingled in a general hubbub, then the firing died down. Rostóv learned later that Russian and Austrian soldiers had been firing at one another.

"My God! What does it all mean?" thought he. "And here, where at any moment the Emperor may see them.... But no, these must be only a handful of scoundrels. It will soon be over, it can't be *that*, it can't be! Only to get past them quicker, quicker!"

The idea of defeat and flight could not enter Rostóv's head. Though he saw French cannon and French troops on the Pratzen Heights just where he had been ordered to look for the commander in chief, he could not, did not wish to, believe *that*.

CHAPTER XVIII

Rostóv had been ordered to look for Kutúzov and the Emperor near the village of Pratzen. But neither they nor a single commanding officer were there, only disorganized crowds of troops of various kinds. He urged on his already weary horse to get quickly past these crowds, but the farther he went the more disorganized they were. The highroad on which he had come out was thronged with *calèches*, carriages of all sorts, and Russian and Austrian soldiers of all arms, some wounded and some not. This whole mass droned and jostled in confusion under the dismal influence of cannon balls flying from the French batteries stationed on the Pratzen Heights.

"Where is the Emperor? Where is Kutúzov?" Rostóv kept asking everyone he could stop, but got no answer from anyone.

At last seizing a soldier by his collar he forced him to answer.

"Eh, brother! They've all bolted long ago!" said the soldier, laughing for some reason and shaking himself free.

Having left that soldier who was evidently drunk, Rostóv stopped the horse of a batman or groom of some important personage and began to question him. The man announced that the Tsar had been driven in a carriage at full speed about an hour before along that very road and that he was dangerously wounded.

"It can't be!" said Rostóv. "It must have been someone else."

"I saw him myself," replied the man with a self-confident smile of derision. "I ought to know the Emperor by now, after the times I've seen him in Petersburg. I saw him just as I see you.... There he sat in the carriage as pale as anything. How they made the four black horses fly! Gracious me, they did rattle past! It's time I knew the Imperial horses and Ilyálványch. I don't think Ilyá drives anyone except the Tsar!"

Rostóv let go of the horse and was about to ride on, when a wounded officer passing by addressed him:

"Who is it you want?" he asked. "The commander in chief? He was killed by a cannon ball—struck in the breast before our regiment."

"Not killed—wounded!" another officer corrected him.

"Who? Kutúzov?" asked Rostóv.

"Not Kutúzov, but what's his name—well, never mind... there are not many left alive. Go that way, to that village, all the commanders are there," said the officer, pointing to the village of Hosjeradek, and he walked on.

Rostóv rode on at a footpace not knowing why or to whom he was now going. The Emperor was wounded, the battle lost. It was impossible to doubt it now. Rostóv rode in the direction pointed out to him, in which he saw turrets and a church. What need to hurry? What was he now to say to the Tsar or to Kutúzov, even if they were alive and unwounded?

"Take this road, your honor, that way you will be killed at once!" a soldier shouted to him. "They'd kill you there!"

"Oh, what are you talking about?" said another. "Where is he to go? That way is nearer."

Rostóv considered, and then went in the direction where they said he would be killed.

"It's all the same now. If the Emperor is wounded, am I to try to save myself?" he thought. He rode on to the region where the greatest number of men had perished in fleeing from Pratzen. The French had not yet occupied that region, and the Russians—the uninjured and slightly wounded—had left it long ago. All about the field, like heaps of manure on well-kept plowland, lay from ten to fifteen dead and wounded to each couple of acres. The wounded crept together in twos and threes and one could hear their distressing screams and groans, sometimes feigned—or so it seemed to Rostóv. He put his horse to a trot to avoid seeing all these suffering men, and he felt afraid—afraid not for his life, but for the courage he needed and which he knew would not stand the sight of these unfortunates.

The French, who had ceased firing at this field strewn with dead and wounded where there was no one left to fire at, on seeing an adjutant riding over it trained a gun on him and fired several shots. The sensation of those terrible whistling sounds and of the corpses around him merged in Rostóv's mind into a single feeling of terror and pity for himself. He remembered his mother's last letter. "What would she feel," thought he, "if she saw me here now on this field with the cannon aimed at me?"

In the village of Hosjeradek there were Russian troops retiring from the field of battle, who though still in some confusion were less disordered. The French cannon did not reach there and the musketry fire sounded far away. Here everyone clearly saw and said that the battle was lost. No one whom Rostóv asked could tell him where the Emperor or Kutúzov was. Some said the report that the Emperor was wounded was correct, others that it was not, and explained the false rumor that had spread by the fact that the Emperor's carriage had really galloped from the field of battle with the pale and terrified Ober-Hofmarschal Count Tolstóy, who had ridden out to the battlefield with others in the Emperor's suite. One officer told Rostóv that he had seen someone from headquarters behind the village to the left, and thither Rostóv rode, not hoping to find anyone but merely to ease his conscience. When he had ridden about two miles and had passed the last of the Russian troops, he saw, near a kitchen garden with a ditch round it, two men on horseback facing the ditch. One with a white plume in his hat seemed familiar to Rostóv; the other on a beautiful chestnut horse (which Rostóv fancied he had seen before) rode up to the ditch, struck his horse with his spurs, and giving it the rein leaped lightly over. Only a little earth crumbled from the bank under the horse's hind hoofs. Turning the horse sharply, he again jumped the ditch, and deferentially addressed the horseman with the white plumes, evidently suggesting that he should do the same. The rider, whose figure seemed familiar to Rostóv and involuntarily riveted his attention, made a gesture of refusal with his head and hand and by that gesture Rostóvinstantly recognized his lamented and adored monarch.

"But it can't be he, alone in the midst of this empty field!" thought Rostóv. At that moment Alexander turned his head and Rostóv saw the beloved features that were so deeply engraved on his memory. The Emperor was pale, his cheeks sunken and his eyes hollow, but the charm, the mildness of his features, was all the greater. Rostóv was happy in the assurance that the rumors about the Emperor being wounded were false. He was happy to be seeing him. He knew that he might and even ought to go straight to him and give the message Dolgorúkov had ordered him to deliver.

But as a youth in love trembles, is unnerved, and dares not utter the thoughts he has dreamed of for nights, but looks around for help or a chance of delay and flight when the longed-for moment comes and he is alone with *her*, so Rostóv, now that he had attained what he had longed for more than anything else in the world, did not know how to approach the Emperor, and a thousand reasons occurred to him why it would be inconvenient, unseemly, and impossible to do so.

"What! It is as if I were glad of a chance to take advantage of his being alone and despondent! A strange face may seem unpleasant or painful to him at this moment of sorrow; besides, what can I say to him now, when my heart fails me and my mouth feels dry at the mere sight of him?" Not one of the innumerable speeches addressed to the Emperor that he had composed in his imagination could he now recall. Those speeches were intended for quite other conditions, they were for the most part to be spoken at a moment of victory and triumph, generally when he was dying of wounds and the sovereign had thanked him for heroic deeds, and while dying he expressed the love his actions had proved.

"Besides how can I ask the Emperor for his instructions for the right flank now that it is nearly four o'clock and the battle is lost? No, certainly I must not approach him, I must not intrude on his reflections. Better die a thousand times than risk receiving an unkind look or bad opinion from him," Rostóv decided; and sorrowfully and with a heart full despair he rode away, continually looking back at the Tsar, who still remained in the same attitude of indecision.

While Rostóv was thus arguing with himself and riding sadly away, Captain von Toll chanced to ride to the same spot, and seeing the Emperor at once rode up to him, offered his services, and assisted him to cross the ditch on foot. The Emperor, wishing to rest and feeling unwell, sat down under an apple tree and von Toll remained beside him. Rostóv from a distance saw with envy and remorse how von Toll spoke long and warmly to the Emperor and how the Emperor, evidently weeping, covered his eyes with his hand and pressed von Toll's hand.

"And I might have been in his place!" thought Rostóv, and hardly restraining his tears of pity for the Emperor, he rode on in utter despair, not knowing where to or why he was now riding.

His despair was all the greater from feeling that his own weakness was the cause of his grief.

He might... not only might but should, have gone up to the sovereign. It was a unique chance to show his devotion to the Emperor and he had not made use of it.... "What have I done?" thought he. And he turned round and galloped back to the place where he had seen the Emperor, but there was no one beyond the ditch now. Only some carts and carriages were passing by. From one of the drivers he learned that Kutúzov's staff were not far off, in the village the vehicles were going to. Rostóv followed them. In front of him walked Kutúzov's groom leading horses in horsecloths. Then came a cart, and behind that walked an old, bandy-legged domestic serf in a peaked cap and sheepskin coat.

"Tit! I say, Tit!" said the groom.

"What?" answered the old man absent-mindedly.

"Go, Tit! Thresh a bit!"

"Oh, you fool!" said the old man, spitting angrily. Some time passed in silence, and then the same joke was repeated.

Before five in the evening the battle had been lost at all points. More than a hundred cannon were already in the hands of the French.

Przebyszéwski and his corps had laid down their arms. Other columns after losing half their men were retreating in disorderly confused masses.

The remains of Langeron's and Dokhtúrov's mingled forces were crowding around the dams and banks of the ponds near the village of Augesd.

After five o'clock it was only at the Augesd Dam that a hot cannonade (delivered by the French alone) was still to be heard from numerous batteries ranged on the slopes of the Pratzen Heights, directed at our retreating forces.

In the rearguard, Dokhtúrov and others rallying some battalions kept up a musketry fire at the French cavalry that was pursuing our troops. It was growing dusk. On the narrow Augesd Dam where for so many years the old miller had been accustomed to sit in his tasseled cap peacefully angling, while his grandson, with shirt sleeves rolled up, handled the floundering silvery fish in the watering can, on that dam over which for so many years Moravians in shaggy caps and blue jackets had peacefully driven their two-horse carts loaded with wheat and had returned dusty with flour whitening their carts—on that narrow dam amid the wagons and the cannon, under the horses' hoofs and between the wagon wheels, men disfigured by fear of death now crowded together, crushing one another, dying, stepping over the dying and killing one another, only to move on a few steps and be killed themselves in the same way.

Every ten seconds a cannon ball flew compressing the air around, or a shell burst in the midst of that dense throng, killing some and splashing with blood those near them.

Dólokhov—now an officer—wounded in the arm, and on foot, with the regimental commander on horseback and some ten men of his company, represented all that was left of that whole regiment. Impelled by the crowd, they had got wedged in at the approach to the dam and, jammed in on all sides, had stopped because a horse in front had fallen under a cannon and the crowd were dragging it out. A cannon ball killed someone behind them, another fell in front and splashed Dólokhov with blood. The crowd, pushing forward desperately, squeezed together, moved a few steps, and again stopped.

"Move on a hundred yards and we are certainly saved, remain here another two minutes and it is certain death," thought each one.

Dólokhov who was in the midst of the crowd forced his way to the edge of the dam, throwing two soldiers off their feet, and ran onto the slippery ice that covered the millpool.

"Turn this way!" he shouted, jumping over the ice which creaked under him; "turn this way!" he shouted to those with the gun. "It bears!..."

The ice bore him but it swayed and creaked, and it was plain that it would give way not only under a cannon or a crowd, but very soon even under his weight alone. The men looked at him and pressed to the bank, hesitating to step onto the ice. The general on horseback at the entrance to the dam raised his hand and opened his mouth to address Dólokhov. Suddenly a cannon ball hissed so low above the crowd that everyone ducked. It flopped into something moist, and the general fell from his horse in a pool of blood. Nobody gave him a look or thought of raising him.

"Get onto the ice, over the ice! Go on! Turn! Don't you hear? Go on!" innumerable voices suddenly shouted after the ball had struck the general, the men themselves not knowing what, or why, they were shouting.

One of the hindmost guns that was going onto the dam turned off onto the ice. Crowds of soldiers from the dam began running onto the frozen pond. The ice gave way under one of the foremost soldiers, and one leg slipped into the water. He tried to right himself but fell in up to his waist. The nearest soldiers shrank back, the gun driver stopped his horse, but from behind still came the shouts: "Onto the ice, why do you stop? Go on! Go on!" And cries of horror were heard in the crowd. The soldiers near the gun waved their arms and beat the horses to make them turn and move on. The horses moved off the bank. The ice, that had held under those on foot, collapsed in a great mass, and some forty men who were on it dashed, some forward and some back, drowning one another.

Still the cannon balls continued regularly to whistle and flop onto the ice and into the water and oftenest of all among the crowd that covered the dam, the pond, and the bank.

CHAPTER XIX

On the Pratzen Heights, where he had fallen with the flagstaff in his hand, lay Prince Andrew Bolkónski bleeding profusely and unconsciously uttering a gentle, piteous, and childlike moan.

Toward evening he ceased moaning and became quite still. He did not know how long his unconsciousness lasted. Suddenly he again felt that he was alive and suffering from a burning, lacerating pain in his head.

"Where is it, that lofty sky that I did not know till now, but saw today?" was his first thought. "And I did not know this suffering either," he thought. "Yes, I did not know anything, anything at all till now. But where am I?"

He listened and heard the sound of approaching horses, and voices speaking French. He opened his eyes. Above him again was the same lofty sky with clouds that had risen and were floating still higher, and between them gleamed blue infinity. He did not turn his head and did not see those who, judging by the sound of hoofs and voices, had ridden up and stopped near him.

It was Napoleon accompanied by two aides-de-camp. Bonaparte riding over the battlefield had given final orders to strengthen the batteries firing at the Augesd Dam and was looking at the killed and wounded left on the field.

"Fine men!" remarked Napoleon, looking at a dead Russian grenadier, who, with his face buried in the ground and a blackened nape, lay on his stomach with an already stiffened arm flung wide.

"The ammunition for the guns in position is exhausted, Your Majesty," said an adjutant who had come from the batteries that were firing at Augesd.

"Have some brought from the reserve," said Napoleon, and having gone on a few steps he stopped before Prince Andrew, who lay on his back with the flagstaff that had been dropped beside him. (The flag had already been taken by the French as a trophy.)

"That's a fine death!" said Napoleon as he gazed at Bolkónski.

Prince Andrew understood that this was said of him and that it was Napoleon who said it. He heard the speaker addressed as *Sire*. But he heard the words as he might have heard the buzzing of a fly. Not only did they not interest him, but he took no notice of them and at once forgot them. His head was burning, he felt himself bleeding to death, and he saw above him the remote, lofty, and everlasting sky. He knew it was Napoleon—his hero—but at that moment Napoleon seemed to him such a small, insignificant creature compared with what was passing now between himself and that lofty infinite sky with the clouds flying over it. At that moment it meant nothing to him who might be standing over him, or what was said of him; he was only glad that people were standing near him and only wished that they would help him and bring him back to life, which seemed to him so beautiful now that he had today learned to understand it so differently. He collected all his strength, to stir and utter a sound. He feebly moved his leg and uttered a weak, sickly groan which aroused his own pity.

"Ah! He is alive," said Napoleon. "Lift this young man up and carry him to the dressing station."

Having said this, Napoleon rode on to meet Marshal Lannes, who, hat in hand, rode up smiling to the Emperor to congratulate him on the victory.

Prince Andrew remembered nothing more: he lost consciousness from the terrible pain of being lifted onto the stretcher, the jolting while being moved, and the probing of his wound at the dressing station. He did not regain consciousness till late in the day, when with other wounded and captured Russian officers he was carried to the hospital. During this transfer he felt a little stronger and was able to look about him and even speak.

The first words he heard on coming to his senses were those of a French convoy officer, who said rapidly: "We must halt here: the Emperor will pass here immediately; it will please him to see these gentlemen prisoners."

"There are so many prisoners today, nearly the whole Russian army, that he is probably tired of them," said another officer.

"All the same! They say this one is the commander of all the Emperor Alexander's Guards," said the first one, indicating a Russian officer in the white uniform of the Horse Guards.

Bolkónski recognized Prince Repnín whom he had met in Petersburg society. Beside him stood a lad of nineteen, also a wounded officer of the Horse Guards.

Bonaparte, having come up at a gallop, stopped his horse.

"Which is the senior?" he asked, on seeing the prisoners.

They named the colonel, Prince Repnín.

"You are the commander of the Emperor Alexander's regiment of Horse Guards?" asked Napoleon.

"I commanded a squadron," replied Repnín.

"Your regiment fulfilled its duty honorably," said Napoleon.

"The praise of a great commander is a soldier's highest reward," said Repnín.

"I bestow it with pleasure," said Napoleon. "And who is that young man beside you?"

Prince Repnín named Lieutenant Sukhtélen.

After looking at him Napoleon smiled.

"He's very young to come to meddle with us."

"Youth is no hindrance to courage," muttered Sukhtélen in a failing voice.

"A splendid reply!" said Napoleon. "Young man, you will go far!"

Prince Andrew, who had also been brought forward before the Emperor's eyes to complete the show of prisoners, could not fail to attract his attention. Napoleon apparently remembered seeing him on the battlefield and, addressing him, again used the epithet "young man" that was connected in his memory with Prince Andrew.

"Well, and you, young man," said he. "How do you feel, *mon brave?*"

Though five minutes before, Prince Andrew had been able to say a few words to the soldiers who were carrying him, now with his eyes fixed straight on Napoleon, he was silent.... So insignificant at that moment seemed to him all the interests that engrossed Napoleon, so mean did his hero himself with his paltry vanity and joy in victory appear, compared to the lofty, equitable, and kindly sky which he had seen and understood, that he could not answer him.

Everything seemed so futile and insignificant in comparison with the stern and solemn train of thought that weakness from loss of blood, suffering, and the nearness of death aroused in him. Looking into Napoleon's eyes Prince Andrew thought of the insignificance of greatness, the unimportance of life which no one could understand, and the still greater unimportance of death, the meaning of which no one alive could understand or explain.

The Emperor without waiting for an answer turned away and said to one of the officers as he went: "Have these gentlemen attended to and taken to my bivouac; let my doctor, Larrey, examine their wounds. *Au revoir*, Prince Repnín!" and he spurred his horse and galloped away.

His face shone with self-satisfaction and pleasure.

The soldiers who had carried Prince Andrew had noticed and taken the little gold icon Princess Mary had hung round her brother's neck, but seeing the favor the Emperor showed the prisoners, they now hastened to return the holy image.

Prince Andrew did not see how and by whom it was replaced, but the little icon with its thin gold chain suddenly appeared upon his chest outside his uniform.

"It would be good," thought Prince Andrew, glancing at the icon his sister had hung round his neck with such emotion and reverence, "it would be good if everything were as clear and simple as it seems to Mary. How good it would be to know where to seek for help in this life, and what to expect after it beyond the grave! How happy and calm I should be if I could now say: 'Lord, have mercy on me!'... But to whom should I say that? Either to a Power indefinable, incomprehensible, which I not only cannot address but which I cannot even express in words—the Great All or Nothing-" said he to himself, "or to that God who has been sewn into this amulet by Mary! There is nothing certain, nothing at all except the unimportance of everything I understand, and the greatness of something incomprehensible but all-important."

The stretchers moved on. At every jolt he again felt unendurable pain; his feverishness increased and he grew delirious. Visions of his father, wife, sister, and future son, and the tenderness he had felt the night before the battle, the figure of the insignificant little Napoleon, and above all this the lofty sky, formed the chief subjects of his delirious fancies.

The quiet home life and peaceful happiness of Bald Hills presented itself to him. He was already enjoying that happiness when that little Napoleon had suddenly appeared with his unsympathizing look of shortsighted delight at the misery of others, and doubts and torments had followed, and only the heavens promised peace. Toward morning all these dreams melted and merged into the chaos and darkness of unconciousness and oblivion which in the opinion of Napoleon's doctor, Larrey, was much more likely to end in death than in convalescence.

"He is a nervous, bilious subject," said Larrey, "and will not recover."

And Prince Andrew, with others fatally wounded, was left to the care of the inhabitants of the district.